MISTAKEN IDENTITY

"Dear God, in heaven!" I gasped. "It's not Daisy, is it? Daisy Whyte?" I had no need for an answer, for I had now recognized my Inverness coat which she had borrowed, and been the proud possessor of, but a short time before.

"Yes, Mrs. Hudson," spoke the constable. "I'm sorry to say it is."

Violet, standing on the periphery of the crowd, her face contorted in anguish, would come no closer. "It's just not right, summat like that happening," she uttered in an emotionally drained voice. "Murdered for a bit of loose change."

Poor Violet. What had been so blatantly clear to me had completely escaped her. Daisy Whyte, a woman of my height and build, wearing my coat and hat, had been done away with in cold blood minutes after emerging from 221B Baker. It doesn't take a Sherlock Holmes—or, if I may be so bold, an Emma Hudson—to see who the intended victim was to have been.

Me.

Other Emma Hudson Mysteries by
Sydney Hosier
from Avon Books

ELEMENTARY, MRS. HUDSON

Murder, Mrs. Hudson

SYDNEY HOSIER

AVON BOOKS ▲ NEW YORK

VISIT OUR WEBSITE AT
http://AvonBooks.com

AVON BOOKS
A division of
The Hearst Corporation
1350 Avenue of the Americas
New York, New York 10019

Copyright © 1997 by Jack Hosier
Published by arrangement with the author
Library of Congress Catalog Card Number: 96-96869
ISBN: 0-380-78176-X

First Avon Books Printing: February 1997

Acknowledgments

With special acknowledgment to Rosalie Williams, Robert and Geraldine Hosier, Harvey Klinger, Carrie Feron, and Anne McKay Thoroman for their faith, interest, and assistance

Contents

Murder, Mrs. Hudson

ONE

A Gentleman Caller

A STREAM OF October sunlight, taking advantage of a break in a partially overcast morning, entered the kitchen through the small window just above the sink. Its waning warmth gave, I'm afraid, a false sense of hope to a slowly wilting geranium perched on the sill. Vi had bought it no more than a fortnight ago but, in her misguided zeal to extend its potted life, had been guilty of overwatering the poor thing. Its eventual demise would be attributable to nothing less than death by drowning. Still, for all her faults, Violet Warner was a good old soul, and we did get on better than I had first anticipated when offering her the opportunity of moving in with me. Fortunately, I have a nice large bedroom off the kitchen which we shared and an equally large front parlor; so it wasn't as if we were constantly stepping on each other's toes, so to speak. And I'll admit it was easier on me having someone else to help share in the chores. Though, I might add, while she at first was quite preoccupied with her newly acquired status in living under the same roof as Mr. Sherlock Holmes and Dr. Watson, she soon settled down into the everyday mundane duties of the household.

And mundane it was. Not since solving the murders at Haddley Hall had we been fortunate in having the opportunity to exercise our wits in anything approaching or equal to, what it seemed to me would be our first and last case. Actually, to be honest, we did have one mystery to solve, and solve it we did. I only mention it to prove we were still quite capable of conducting an investigation to its final conclusion. It occurred not long after Violet had moved into my (if I may be forgiven) somewhat celebrated address at 221B Baker Street. A neighbor, Mrs. Armitedge by name, had asked us to look into the disappearance of her husband, whom she had neither seen nor heard from for a good three days. The police, we were informed, had made the usual inquiries, but it had all come to naught. Mr. A remained a missing person, while the poor woman, suspecting foul play, was quite beside herself with grief. As it turned out, Violet and I, after conducting extensive interviews with a number of the missing man's old cronies, learned that Mr. Henry Armitedge had, without so much as a by-your-leave, sailed off to Canada with a certain Miss Dolly Hepplewhite, leaving behind, to fend for themselves, Mrs. A and her four small children, thank you very much.

Other than that, nothing, except for noting, with a slight twinge of resentment, that there

seemed to be no lack of clients for a certain upstairs gentleman boarder. Perhaps Dr. Watson
was right when he so forcefully stated, when I
first revealed, to both him and Mr. Holmes, our
involvement in the Haddley affair, "that a
woman's place is in the home and not out gallivanting about the countryside chasing down
murderers." As for Mr. Holmes's reaction, it
was, as I recall, typical of the man—a simple
shrug of the shoulders accompanied by that infuriating enigmatic smile of his that revealed
nothing yet said everything.

Ah, well, I sighed to myself, no use feeling
sorry for yourself, old girl. A nice cup of tea
will soon set things right. No sooner had I filled
the kettle than there came a knocking at the
front door. Now who could that be, I wondered. Surely not Vi, back from the greengrocer
already. Besides, she has her own key in any
event. Setting the kettle aside, I hurried down
the hallway, pausing but momentarily in front
of the small oval-framed mirror in the vestibule
for a brief primping of hair before opening the
door.

"Good day to you, madam. I'm here to see a
Mr. Sherlock Holmes."

Standing before me was a pleasant, though
rather plump-faced young man of medium
height, I should say, smartly turned out in a
light gray frock coat, handsome walking stick,
and bowler. A gentleman, indeed. Though,
what impressed me most about him was his
complexion—smooth and pink, like that of a
child.

"Do you have an appointment?" I asked, opening the door a little farther.

A nod. "For eleven o'clock," he stated. In that instant the old grandfather clock from within the front parlor awoke from its sixty-minute slumber to sound out the hour, accompanied, in turn, by the cuckoo clock in the kitchen. It was a gift Mr. Holmes had brought back for me from a recent trip to the Black Forest. It was quite unlike him, I must say. And while I'm not, to be perfectly honest, partial to cuckoo clocks, I remember thanking him most profusely. Although, what on earth ever possessed him to buy such a thing in the first place, I shall never know.

"You see, madam," smiled the gentleman caller, taking note of the cacophony of chirps and chimes, "if nothing else, I'm punctual."

I returned the smile as he entered. "Your coat and hat?"

"Perhaps just the hat and stick. I shan't be too long," he answered, removing the bowler to reveal a nice crop of sandy red hair.

"Just up the stairs then, if you please, Mr. . . . ?" I paused, waiting for a name, but received nothing more than a clearing of the throat which, if truth be told, sounded more like a growl. With Mr. Holmes receiving a goodly number of visitors over the years who, for reasons of their own, prefer anonymity to all but *that* singular gentleman, it was, I admit, a faux pas on my part. "Yes, right then," said I, trying to make the best of it before once more retiring to my kitchen. "Up the stairs, first door on your right."

By the time I finished my second cup Vi had returned from her marketing mumbling and grumbling about the expense of trying to keep food on the table, what with prices being what they are. "Just at look at this," she announced, uncovering a leg of mutton from its brown-paper wrapping. "Very nice, I'll grant you, but I swear, Emma Hudson, I could have sailed back from Australia with a sheep under me arm for the price I paid for it."

"I don't know where it will all end," I sighed in commiseration. "Oh, by the way," I added as an afterthought, "I was thinking of heating up the shepherd's pie for tonight's supper. What do you think?"

"Yes, that would be nice, Em. Dr. Watson does love his shepherd's pie, don't he? As for his Nibs," she continued, casting an eye upward, "you could give him anything, you could. Eats like a bird, he does."

"Speaking of birds," I said, smiling, "I doubt very much if Mr. Holmes would so much as bat an eye if I were to set before him a certain cuckoo served up in brown gravy."

"Aye," responded my companion with a hearty chuckle. "He's a queer one alright, and no mistake."

"You know," I mused, "I've always had the feeling Mr. Holmes, when he at last steps through the Pearly Gates, will take God to task for having fashioned mankind in such a way that the body, in order to survive, must spend a goodly portion of its life span in the nonproductive act of eating. Time, he would say, that could have best been served pursuing intellectual endeavors rather than culinary repasts."

"You know what I think?" replied Vi. Unfortunately, or otherwise, I never did receive an answer, for my companion had cut short her response and was staring questioningly toward the kitchen door. " 'Ere, now," she blurted out, "where did you come from?" At this unexpected turn in the conversation I eased halfway round in my chair to see framed within the doorway the sandy-haired gentleman caller.

"I didn't mean to disturb you ladies," was the apologetic response. "I simply wish to speak to Mrs. Hudson. You, madam, I take it," he continued, focusing his attention toward me, "are she?"

"Walked right in off ruddy street then, did you?" Vi retorted before I had a chance to speak up. "It's quite alright, Vi," I soothed. "I let this gentleman in earlier to see Mr. Holmes. Yes," I answered, rising from the table to face him, "I'm Mrs. Hudson. What can I do for you?"

"Mr. Holmes thought it might be worth my while to have a word with you," he replied from his position within the doorway.

"Come in, then," I beckoned. As Vi removed his topcoat and left to deposit it in the hall closet, I slid a kitchen chair out from the table and requested he take a seat. As he eased himself down I took my place opposite him across the table.

"You'll have to excuse me for being a bit sharp with you, like," Vi apologized, reentering the kitchen and setting about filling of the kettle. "It's just that in this house a body can't be too careful. Get all kinds, we do, traipsin' in at all hours of the night and day. From toffs like you to gaggles of street urchins and everyone else in between.

"Now then," she added with a smile, "what would you say to a nice cuppa and an iced bun?"

"The thing of it is," he replied, a trifle uncomfortably, "I was hoping for a word or two with Mrs. Hudson."

"I understand what you're saying," I readily assured him. "And if it is of a confidential nature, do not hesitate to speak freely. Mrs. Warner is my trusted companion and privy to whatever information may pass between us."

"In that case," spoke the young man, breaking into a smile, "I believe I will have that cup of tea. And, if the offer still stands, a bun or two, Mrs. Warner? Now then," he went on, as we all settled down to our tea, "as I was saying . . ."

"One moment, if you please," I cut in. "Before we proceed any farther, perhaps you might like to introduce yourself."

"Have I not?" was the startled response from that pink, cherubic face.

"You have not, sir," I smiled.

"My apologies, madam. The name," he replied, while deftly removing from its plate a vanilla-iced bun, "is Churchill. Winston Churchill."

"Churchill," announced Vi, speaking the word aloud very thoughtfully. "Yes!" she exclaimed, "I know that name. Write articles for the *Morning Post*, you do, right?" A smile and a nod confirmed her allegation. "A reporter!"

was the excited response. "Come to do a story on Emma and me then, have you?"

The young man, caught off guard by Vi's remark, looked somewhat bemused if not embarrassed. "Mr. Churchill, my dear, Mrs. Warner," I hastily informed her, "is more than just a reporter. His father, Lord Randolph, before his untimely death, had been in his day chancellor of the Exchequer and was thought by many at the time to be England's next prime minister. And," I went on, addressing myself to our visitor, "if my memory for history serves me right, you, sir, are also a direct descendant of the first duke of Marlborough." He graciously allowed I was right on all counts.

"A pleasure to meet you, Mr. Churchill," I said.

"Likewise, I'm sure," spoke Vi, adding, "I'd curtsy, I would, if I weren't sitting down."

"Good heavens, madam," chortled the young man, "no need for that. I'm not royalty. Now then," he continued, in a more serious vein, "to get down to the business at hand. As I mentioned earlier, I spoke to Mr. Holmes in regard to a certain task I wished him to carry out. One that requires immediate attention. Unfortunately, I was informed by that gentleman that his work schedule, being what it is at present, would make it impossible for him to take on the assignment. Nevertheless, Mr. Holmes did put forward your name as a likely candidate for the job. I was, I confess, quite taken aback at the suggestion and inquired if he were playing me for the fool. 'A woman, indeed!' I thundered." He halted abruptly in his narrative to survey the two somewhat chagrined female faces opposite him. "Ah . . . well, yes," he stammered in obvious embarrassment. "Nothing personal, you understand, ladies," he hastened to inform us.

Oh, yes, thought I, the very idea of a woman believing she had brains enough to step into a position reserved exclusively for the male species would surely set the earth spinning counterclockwise in its orbit. "We understand perfectly," I answered through clenched teeth and forced smile.

"However," he continued, "the gentleman readily assured me that you, dear lady, are also in this detective business. Is that true?"

To say I was flattered that Mr. Holmes had suggested my name would be an understatement to say the very least. Perhaps on some points I had misjudged him. Suppressing my delight, I answered, in what I considered to be a most businesslike tone, that I have from time to time participated in one or two ventures in company with my associate, Mrs. Warner. His reply was no more than a grunt, followed by an interval of brooding silence. Was he having second thoughts? I hoped not. Things had, as I say, been much too quiet of late within the Baker Street residence, and I knew Violet, as well as myself, would favor an interesting diversion. Yet I sensed in Mr. Churchill there still remained certain doubts as to our capabilities. With respect to Mr. Holmes, it was his decision and his alone, not the client's, as to whether he would accept a case or not. Embarrassingly, I found myself in the reverse position, waiting for an affirmative reply from the gentleman seated opposite. I decided to go on the offensive. "This task you speak of," I began, in a casual manner. "Before I, along with Mrs. Warner, decide to take it on, we would have to know just what the assignment entails."

I received a quizzical, then a knowing smile. He knew the game I was playing. "Touché," he replied appreciatively, with a slight bow of the head. Then: "It is nothing, madam, I assure you, that would endanger life or limb. Simply a mere surveillance of a certain gentleman. Although I use the word 'gentleman' not in the literal sense."

"A bad lot then, is he?" quizzed Vi.

"You might say that, Mrs. Warner," came the reply. "You might, indeed."

"But," I queried, "you say, Mr. Churchill, a surveillance? Nothing more?" I must admit I was a bit disappointed. I could now see why Mr. H had suddenly acquired "a heavy work schedule." No, Sherlock Holmes was not one to spend his time hiding behind a streetlamp or peering round corners. The unearthing of a clue, explaining the unexplainable crime, the thrill of the hunt, this is what the good detective relished.

"Yes," was the young man's reply, "just find out who he sees, where he goes, that type of thing."

It would seem we had our assignment. Yet his answer did not sit well with me. It belied a forced casualness.

"Do you have any objections?" he asked, bringing forth a cigar from an inside coat pocket. "Perhaps the smoke and all . . ."

"Smoke away, if you've a mind to," acknowledged Violet. "Dirty habit though it is. 'Ere," she added, "you can use the saucer for an ashtray. I'll just pop it in the sink along with the rest of the dishes when you're through."

"If you're sure . . ."

"Now, don't you go frettin' yourself, luv," she continued, in motherly fashion. "If all we had to worry about was a bit of cigar smoke, we'd be nowt but happy. Should have been here last week, you should, eh, Em?"

"I'm sure, Violet, that Mr. Churchill isn't—"

"Had a ruddy explosion, we did," continued Vi, completely ignoring me. "Them two, again"—she gestured with thumb toward the ceiling—"workin' on some kind of experiment, they were, when all of a sudden, boom! Scared the bloomin' life out of me, it did. Should have seen their room! There, lyin' in the corner was General Kitchener . . ."

"Good, God, madam!" cried Churchill, with mouth agape. "Not General Kitchener!"

"Aye, well, it were a photograph of him, like. With the picture glass and frame all smashed and half the walls blackened by smoke. Took us a good two days or more to clean the flamin' room up. Em will tell you, right enough."

"Yes, Violet," I echoed in exasperation, "a good two days. Now, then, Mr. Churchill," said I, turning my attention back to our visitor, "I don't wish to belabor the point, but with respect to the surveillance of which you spoke, I believe you're not being altogether truthful with me. If

I am to be of service to you, I must be made aware of all the facts."

"You are quite perceptive, madam," he replied, with a deft flick of ash into saucer, "and I shall try to be as forthcoming as possible in regard to what information I possess."

With jaw jutting slightly forward and fleshy bottom lip set firmly within that boyish face, he presented a quite serious mien. Yet, resting the cigar in the saucer and tilting back in his chair with the now unbuttoned suit coat making the waistcoat accessible for thumbs to be jauntily tucked into the two small fob pockets, he looked every bit the London dandy. A many-faceted character, indeed. And, I would say, a much more complex individual than would be imagined in a man of his twenty-odd years.

"What I can tell you," he began, "is that the so-called gentleman in question is known to law enforcement agencies throughout Europe simply as Marcos. Actual nationality unknown. A shadowy figure at best, madam, whose nefarious deeds, I might add, are available to the highest bidder."

"A hired thug, is he? Leastways, that's what the Americans would call him," Vi cut in, exhibiting her knowledge of Crime Americana gleaned from the perusal of too many penny dreadfuls from overseas.

"A hired thug," repeated Mr. Churchill with a smile. "Yes, I like that. Though, with a list of crimes ranging from bombings to assassinations, it would, I think, elevate him to a somewhat higher classification within the criminal hierarchy."

"Bombings, you say! An anarchist, then?" I asked.

"I would not call him so," he answered, before blowing lightly to fan the embered tip of his cigar. "An anarchist is someone with a political point of view, however deranged or misguided it may be. Our friend Marcos is without political leanings one way or the other. Greed is his god. Murder, his mistress, and the world can go to hell in a handbasket for all he cares."

"And the ruddy beggar's never been caught?" put in Vi.

"Once," he answered. "In Brussels. Picked up in connection with an attempted assassination of a top government official but escaped custody within twenty-four hours." At that, he reached into an inside coat pocket and extracted a sheaf of paper. "However," he went on, "as luck would have it, a certain Belgian constable possessing an artistic flair was able to make a rough sketch of him from memory. Although, I might add, he is a well-known figure within the underworld on both sides of the Channel. This is a copy," he announced, laying it before me, "of the only known picture of him to exist within police files."

The charcoal sketch showed a full mane of black hair combed straight back from a broad, brooding forehead. Eyebrows that continued their way across the bridge of a prominent nose, formed an overhang for the dead, deep-set cavernous eyes beneath them. A thick scraggle of a moustache and a strong chin line completed the picture. It was an angry face. It was a determined face. It was an evil face. I passed it along for Vi's inspection. "Oh, I don't like the look of him!" She shuddered.

Then I put forward two questions to the young man across the table. "What leads you to believe he is now in England, Mr. Churchill? And what," I added, "would his purpose be on this side of the Channel?"

"I have information from a certain official within Scotland Yard, whose name I need not mention," we were informed, "that our friend, Marcos, is believed to have been seen by one or two individuals within our criminal society frequenting various alehouses along the waterfront. If indeed it is the gentleman in question," he went on, pausing only long enough to inspect his now empty cup, "it would be logical to assume he has lodgings within the area."

" 'Ere," announced Vi, having caught the obvious ploy in regard to the empty cup, "I'll just fill that up for you, will I?"

"Very kind of you." He smiled. "You make an excellent brew, Mrs. Warner," he added thoughtfully after a sip or two. "Not a blend, but, (another sip) Ceylon, is it?"

"Right as rain, you are, Mr. Churchill." She laughed. "Know your tea, you do."

"Not as well as I know my sherry," was the equally hearty response. Then, turning his attention back to me, he continued, "His purpose, you ask, Mrs. Hudson? Consider this—the man works on an international level. Combine that thought with England's present military situation in South Africa."

"South Africa!" I cried out in astonishment.

"Are you saying his arrival is connected in some way with the Boer War?"

"The Boer War now, is it!" exclaimed Violet before a reply could be given. "At first, it was nowt but a mere surveillance. Now," complained my companion with little or no discretion with respect to our still somewhat hesitant client, "we're into assassins, the Boers, and who knows what else. Play with words, you do, Mr. Churchill. It's a wonder you never entered politics."

"Vi, really...."

"That's quite alright, Mrs. Hudson," he interceded. "I can well understand Mrs. Warner's consternation. The thing of it is," he continued, addressing Vi, "all of this is but supposition. The man spotted may not be Marcos at all. If it should prove otherwise, he may be over here simply cooling his heels 'til things quiet down for him 'cross the Channel. So you see," he added, with twinkled eye and a wagging of a stubby forefinger, "I was not being altogether untruthful after all. Still, in all honesty, I hear rumors are running rampant at the Yard that the man has been brought over here by someone in sympathy with the Boers to, in effect, bring the war to England's shores. Should that be the case, his presence could well be a prelude to a planned assassination, a series of bombings, or even the kidnapping of a government official, perhaps the prime minister himself or a member of the Royal household."

Violet and I exchanged skeptical glances, believing, as we did, that Mr. Churchill, well intentioned though he might be, was the possessor of a most fanciful imagination. Prime minister and Royal household, indeed. Be that as it may, I nodded in thoughtful agreement to all that was said.

"As for your mention of politics, Mrs. Warner," he continued, eyeing the last remaining bun, "the Churchillian hat has already been thrown into that ring during the last by-election in Oldham."

"Oh," confessed Vi, "I didn't know."

"Nor, would it seem," he chuckled, as a paw of a hand swooped down to retrieve the solitary morsel, "did many of the good people of Oldham. I lost."

"Oh, I am sorry."

"No matter, Mrs. Warner. 'Tis a battle lost, not the war."

"Speaking of wars," I ventured, "I find it a sad commentary on our times that on the threshold of a new century, we should find ourselves in foreign battlefields after so many years of peace."

"Foreign battlefields, madam?" he remarked sharply, with emphasis on the word "foreign." "Did you say 'foreign' battlefields? The territories of South Africa," he declared, "are and will always be a part of the British Empire. I tell you this," he continued in a more forceful manner than ever he had exhibited since his arrival. "It will take more than roving bands of Boer farmers to oust Her Majesty's forces from the tip of Africa!"

"Well, if you'll pardon me for saying so," spoke Vi, "from what I read in the papers we haven't been doing all that well of late. Mind you," she quickly added, "I'm not sayin' our lads aren't doin' their bit. God luv 'em."

"I'll not deny," he continued on most aggressively, with the slight lisp with which he was afflicted becoming more pronounced as he forced out the words, "that we've had our setbacks. If the Boers were professional soldiers and fought in classic battle formation, this business would have been over months ago, with England the victor. But, no," he added in much the same agitated manner, "they fight in small groups—hit-and-run tactics—never know where they'll strike next. Commandos, they call themselves. Commandos," he repeated, suddenly breaking off his tirade. "Now that I think about it, a good word, that," he announced, more to himself, I think, than to his faithful audience of two. "Forgive me, ladies," he stated from across the table. "I am what you might call a collector of words. There are those that collect stamps. Others, butterflies. I, as I say, am a word collector. Commandos," he repeated the word once more, adding, "I shall have to store that away up here"—he gestured with a tap to the forehead—"for future use."

Thinking back on that conversation round the kitchen table, I thought at the time that war, or the talk of it, was the catalyst to unlocking the man's emotions. Did we have before us a frustrated present-day duke of Marlborough, who, with no men to lead or wars to command, continued to run off in all directions looking for his own particular path of destiny? And were we to be dragged along that path with him? Be that as it may, the task he had set before us I judged to be, at best, routine, no more so than the Armitedge affair. Notwithstanding Mr. Churchill's ramblings of prime ministers being assassinated or members of the monarchy being kidnapped. Put simply, we were to find out if there was indeed a "Marcos" frequenting the area along the waterfront and, if such was the case, locate his lodgings, put him under surveillance, and report our findings back to our client. But where, precisely, to start? "When you speak of his having been seen on the waterfront, Mr. Churchill," I asked, "of what area are you speaking? The Surrey Dock? The Royal? East India, or . . . ?"

"The London Dock, madam," he answered with a few last puffs on the slowly diminishing cigar. "I'm sorry I can't be of more assistance than that."

"Well, it's a help, at least," Vi knowingly informed him. "Know the area, we do. Though it's been a good many years since we were down there."

I had one question remaining. "I wonder," said I, putting it to him somewhat hesitantly, "just what your interest is in all this? Other than," I quickly added, "your duty as an Englishman in time of conflict." I was afforded a wisp of a smile before receiving my reply.

"I write, as you know," he began, "articles on a freelance basis for the *Morning Post*. As such, I would not, how shall I say, be averse to the international publicity to be gained in that newspaper by exposing a plot against the PM or a member of the Royal family. It's as simple as that, I'm afraid." He shrugged.

"You seek to make a name for yourself?" was my bewildered response. "But, surely, the name, Churchill, in itself . . ."

"Oh, the name Churchill, is quite well-known, I grant you that," he cut in, squashing in the process the remains of his cigar into the saucer (not one of my best, thank goodness). "Young Churchill, yes, I know the lad," he spoke, playing out the words as would an actor in a play. "William, isn't it? Or," he went on, in much the same theatrical vein, "Churchill? Oh, yes, the late Lord Randolph's son, you mean? You see, madam"—he gestured hopelessly—"it's never *Winston* Churchill."

"Your point is well taken, Mr. *Winston* Churchill." I smiled.

" 'Pon my word, Mrs. Hudson!" he roared in good-natured laughter. "You are, as Mrs. Warner would say, 'a bit of alright, you are.' "

"And many the times I've said those very words," was Vi's appreciative reply.

"Nevertheless, sir," I ventured, in light-hearted fashion, "methinks the gentleman doth protest too much."

"Perhaps," he admitted with a smile. "But only to make a point. It's true," he added, "I've made a mark in sociopolitical circles, including the military. But circles, madam, at best, no larger than the circumference of London."

"And you," I put the question to him in the form of a statement, "seek acclaim on the grand scale."

"Acclaim?" He paused for a moment to digest the thought before adding, "That sounds rather pompous, doesn't it? Say rather, recog-

nition. The thing of it is," he confided to us with
obvious reference to the Oldham defeat, "I'm
not finished with politics yet. I have long-range
plans for that particular arena."

No doubt, thought I, they would include the
eventual capture of the office that had eluded
his father.

After a fee was discussed and an amicable
agreement reached, he rose from his chair.
"And now, ladies," he announced, "I must be
off. I thank you both for your time and your
tea."

I was left to wonder aloud as I escorted our
new client down the hallway, whether he had
expounded to Mr. Holmes in as great detail as
with Vi and me, his assumption that an alleged
terrorist could, at this moment, be walking the
streets of London.

"No, I didn't, actually," he confessed. "I
thought it best at the time to parcel out only
that information which I considered pertinent
to a surveillance. Perhaps," he added thoughtfully, "if I had . . ." He let the thought hang
before announcing in his hearty fashion, "Nevertheless, Mrs. Hudson, you may rest assured
that I have every confidence in both you and
Mrs. Warner." It was a gallant remark, however
true or untrue it may have been. "In any event,
dear lady," he added in parting, before slipping
into his coat and taking leave down a much
congested Baker Street, "I shall call within the
week to see what progress you have made."

I hurried back down the hall, anxious to find
out what Vi had thought of our young Mr.

Churchill. As I entered the kitchen I was taken aback by the sight of my companion with yet another cup in hand. "Good, heavens, Mrs. Warner," I cried out in mock admonishment, "not more tea! You'll be floating, you will."

"It's not tea," I was duly informed as she advanced toward the luckless geranium, which seemed to cringe in terror at her approach. "Poor little thing," she clucked sympathetically while emptying the contents of the cup into the soil, "looks half-dead. Needs a good waterin', it does."

TWO

Paddy O'Ryan, Himself

∾ As I HAD been asked by Mr. Churchill to present whatever I had been able to unearth before week's end, I had hoped to have at least some tidbit of news to pass along. However, I have to admit that by the following Thursday we had succeeded in obtaining absolutely no information whatsoever with regard to a sighting or the whereabouts of the man known simply as Marcos.

On our sojourns into the various watering holes along the waterfront, I would confront the publicans and their seedy array of customers with the story that Vi and I were sisters in search of a long-lost brother. At this point I would unfurl the charcoal sketch in the hope of receiving a sign of recognition from the befuddled brains and bloodshot eyes of our audience. For our little act, we received, for the most part, no more than a light scan of the picture, coupled with a negative shaking of heads, before backs were turned and we, along with the picture, were forgotten.

And so it was that for the fifth time in as many days, we found ourselves once more approaching the area of Wapping, site of the London Dock. With a signal to our driver to stop, we alighted from the cab onto Radcliffe. From there, our walk took us south down Pennington Street, where, once again, we passed through neighborhoods, to put it kindly, not frequented by the tourist. Nor should they be. I doubted whether very little had changed all that much since the time of Dickens, whose Artful Dodger I half expected to see scurrying down some twisted alley.

From the street, one could see above the sagging rooftops of shops huddled together in tired desperation the towering tips of timbered masts from the tall ships berthed at dockside. For two women whose late husbands had both sailed and served on such ships, it was a sight to stir old memories. However, the bite of an October wind coupled with damp air set us quickening our pace past the locals, who eyed us with furtive glances. All, that is, save one. An old salt, with mouth agape forming a little "o" within an abundantly white (albeit tobacco-stained) beard, lay dead to the world within the doorway of an abandoned shop. Not even the sound of two dappled drays with a wagonload of fine old kegs clomping over cobbled stone caused him to stir in the slightest from his inebriated slumber.

On turning the corner, a sullen, sallow-faced young woman approaching from the opposite direction, with but a tattered shawl for protection against an intermittent spattering of rain, appraised the two of us from head to toe in no more than a flick of an eye and, just as quickly and as silently, passed.

"Look like the aristocracy to this lot, we do," was Vi's wry comment on the scene.

In truth, I had to admit she was right. Although, I should add, with Vi's coat, a full-length tweed chesterfield that had seen a good three winters, and I, in a sensible though slightly worn three-quarter rainproof, we weren't, in any sense of the word, dressed to the nines. "It would seem," I noted, "that we have not, as I had hoped, downplayed our garb to the level of our surroundings."

"Aye," she agreed. "Seems it takes summat less than a serviceable coat or two or," she added with an eye toward my hat, "the removal of feathers from a toque before we'd be accepted down here as next-door neighbors."

I had taken pains to remove the array of egret feathers of which she spoke, in the belief it would offer a less ostentatious display of finery. Yet, with hindsight, I realized a simple toque of crushed velvet would appear as unattainable as the crown of England to women with naught but tattered shawls.

It was at this point in thought that I suddenly felt a slight tug at my sleeve. Startled, I gazed down to see a tyke of no more than eight or nine years staring up at me with saucer blue eyes set within an angelic, if somewhat slightly smudged, face. "Well, who have we here?" I smiled.

"Please, missus," he blurted out with extended hand palm up, "could you spare a shilling for a poor boy what's got no mum?"

"No, mum!" exclaimed Violet in motherly concern. "Why, however do you live, lad?"

We waited but received no answer. Instead, the tousled head was cast downward as two little feet shuffled awkwardly about within a pair of oversize, laceless boots. After an interval of silence from all sides, the small grubby hand was once more extended. "Please, missus. Missus?" he repeated, this time turning his attention to Violet in the hope of enlarging his sum by two. His wish was not to be denied. As two sets of gloved fingers began a search through leathered purses, a voice rang out from behind.

"Alright, alright, 'op it, Sunshine!"

Looming just to the back of us, at a good six feet in height, stood a most formidable bushy-bearded officer of the law. With his having arrived on the scene as if out of nowhere, I'm afraid we literally jumped at the sound of the voice that boomed out from above.

"'Pon, my word, Constable," said I, emitting a slight gasp, "you gave us quite a start."

"Sorry, madam," he answered, with a smart two-finger salute to the brimmed helmet. "It's the tyke I was trying to put the fear of the law into."

"Why?" exclaimed Violet in minor outrage. "What's he done, eh? Little lad like that. Why, he's . . . why, wherever did he go?" she asked, looking round just in time to catch the backside of our disappearing angel hightailing it down the street. "Only wanted a shilling, poor thing," she fretted. "And him what's got no mum."

"No mum, is it?" remarked the constable with a smile. "Was that his story?"

"But, surely, Officer," I spoke up in defense of the boy, "there was no harm in . . ."

"Give to one and you'll find yourself surrounded by his lot and more," we were dutifully informed. "Now, if I may be so bold as to ask," he went on, with clasped hands behind that ramrod back, "what are you two ladies doing here?"

"Here?" I repeated, while mentally trying to fashion an answer that would satisfy the both of us. To admit we were looking for an international terrorist who might or might not even be in the country (let alone Wapping) would, I'm afraid, only complicate the situation even more.

"Here," he stated once more. "You're not from these parts," he added in a smug tone. "I should know that if you were."

"Charity," announced Vi.

The beady eyes beneath the brim quickly focused in on my companion. "Eh?" he asked. "How's that, again?"

"Charity," she repeated, this time clarifying her answer by adding, "We're down here doin' our bit for charity, like."

I picked up on her story. "Yes, that's it," I stammered in flustered response, "we're helping out. Ah, volunteer work, you might say." I gulped nervously, grateful that the female of the species is not endowed with an Adam's apple to bob up and down in telltale anxiety. Why is it I find it so difficult to lie to anyone in authority?

"I see," was the slow, drawn-out reply, as a hand lightly stroked the growth of beard below the chin line. "Charity, you say? And what church would you be doing this charity for?"

Obviously he hadn't made up his mind whether to believe us or not. We had no idea of any church within the vicinity.

"It's not for church," Violet blithely informed him. "It's for the Army."

"The army!" the poor man blurted out in complete bewilderment. "Here, now," he demanded to know, "what kind of a game are you two playing?"

"Why, you big lummock," she addressed the officer in good-natured laughter. "Have you never heard of the *Salvation* Army?"

"The Salvation Army, is it?" (A satisfied smile.) "A right good lot, they are."

"Indeed they are, Constable," I concurred. "Actually, we're to meet a Sergeant Watson of the Army" (I was sure the good doctor wouldn't mind my borrowing his name) "at one of the common lodging houses, you know, for the handing out of pamphlets, that type of thing." Having spotted just such an establishment across the street with its wooden shingle proclaiming J. Shandling's Lodging House, I added, "We're to meet at the Shandling House. Perhaps you've heard of it? I believe it's somewhere in the vicinity."

I must have been more convincing with my story this time, for he allowed, with a hearty chuckle emanating from somewhere deep within that forest of facial hair that "if we were any closer to it, we'd be inside." After having it dutifully pointed it out to us, we graciously thanked him for all his help and left him to his patrol.

"Careful where you step, Vi," I advised, with a slight hitch to my hemline as we proceeded across the street. "What with the horses. . . ." I let the sentence hang, no further explanation being needed. Once on the other side, Violet let out a cry of despair. "It's gone!" she wailed, while hands began a frantic search within the pockets of her coat.

"Why, whatever is the matter? What's gone?"

"Me lace-edged handkerchief," she moaned. "It was in me pocket when we left the house. I know it was."

"Yes," I agreed. "I remember seeing the tip of it sticking out just before the young lad approached." No sooner had I spoken the words than a mental picture of what I believed happened flashed before me. I broke out in a peal of laughter.

"'Ere," came the angry protest, "it's nowt to laugh at!"

"I'm sorry, Vi," I apologized, stifling a giggle. "I was just thinking how happy Mr. Dickens would be in knowing the Artful Dodger is alive and well and living in Wapping."

"The Artful Dodger?"

"Never mind, dear," I answered with a gentle pat to her arm. "Let's check out the lodging, shall we?"

On entering, we found the communal kitchen, or eating area of the establishment, to be a dismal place indeed, with its floorboards, walls, and low-slung ceiling of charred and grimy oak—no doubt the salvaged remains of some long-forgotten fire-gutted ship, beached and left to rot among the dunes.

Looking for somewhere to seat ourselves, we bypassed the rows of long wooden tables and benches, opting for at least a limited degree of privacy by selecting the partitioned areas of smaller tables and backless chairs along the wall. As the open fireplace at the far end of the room, with dying embers emitting hissing and spitting noises like some caged reptilian creature offered up little or no warmth, we were obliged to remain seated in our coats. In all likelihood, the more prudent course of action.

Taking in our surroundings while in the process of endlessly wafting away billows of cheap tobacco smoke, I noted there were only three other women present besides ourselves. The rest, a collection of dockhands, stevedores, and warehouse workers who, no doubt, were laid off or unemployed, sought solace for themselves amid drink and companionship. Wending his way in beaded perspiration through that haze of smoke, loud conversation, and even louder laughter, a waiter of rotund proportion with flabby jowls encased on either side by a set of graying mutton-chop sideburns and whose girth encompassed a dirty, grease-stained apron, balanced a tray on which resided a plate of peas, a clump of potatoes, and a heavy-crusted meat pie. Stopping to set it down at the table of an old man across the way, he received no more than a grunt of thanks before departing. I hunched myself up the better to see, as the fellow took knife and fork to pie.

"Oh, I don't like the look of that," I grimaced.

"I don't like the *smell* of it," commented Vi.

"If that meat pie is any indication of the food served here, perhaps it's best," I advised, "if we just order a drink and wait 'til we're home for something to eat."

"Aye, I suppose you're right, luv," she reluctantly agreed. "Though I've a stomach what's already got the collywobbles."

"Better not fed, than dead," I remarked with a smile.

"Better not—? Oh, you're a caution, you are, Emma Hudson. We'll have to send that little saying to our word collector, Mr. Churchill, we will."

"Speaking of Mr. Churchill," I answered, ignoring the barb, "I'm afraid we'll have to have something more than a saying for him if we wish to keep him on as a client."

"Aye, well, I think all this Marcos business is nowt but a wild-goose chase, meself," stated Vi, after having caught the waiter's eye and placed an order for two glasses of stout.

"It could very well be," I confessed. "Nevertheless, we are getting paid to do a job, and it's only right we continue on until Mr. Churchill decides to terminate it."

"Well, the sooner the better, if you ask me. This here ain't exactly Haddley Hall."

"True," I smiled. "But we're not in a position to choose client or location." Still, I had to admit she was right. It was a dreadful area. Not at all the way I remembered it. "The chandlery," I announced, referring to the maritime supply shop that our late husbands had both owned and operated, "couldn't have been too far from here."

"Doubt if it's still there," she mused. "That were a good many years ago."

"Yes," I agreed. "Still, I don't recall the area as being as run-down as it is now. I remember back then it was more, well, colorful, more hustle, more bustle. And the times we had! Why, I can remember—" I stopped on seeing an odd little smile emerge opposite me. "What is it?" I asked.

"Memory sometime wears a pretty frock, Em."

I said no more.

Our rotund waiter, who may have been J. Shandling himself, for all we knew, threaded his way back to our table. "Here you go, ducks," he announced, with the fleshy face breaking into a gap-toothed smile. "Don't get many of your lot down here," was the added comment, as one hand gave the table a quick once-over with the bottom half of the apron while the other deposited our drinks before us.

It was the perfect opening, and I took advantage of it. "The thing of it is," I stated, removing the scrolled picture from my purse, "we're looking for our brother. He's not well, you see. Suffers from loss of memory. We've been told he may be in the area. Perhaps you—" I unrolled the picture.

"Your brother, you say?" he asked, after a silent moment of study.

"Yes," we chorused, eagerly awaiting an affirmative reply.

"No," came the answer on the picture's return to the table, "I've not seen that face in here. Sorry, ducks." And, like the aforementioned "ducks," he waddled off.

"Well," announced Vi, with a despairing sigh, "that were a letdown."

"Not to worry," said I, trying to make the best of it. "We'll just finish our drinks and then make the rounds of the tables. We may find somebody in here yet who remembers seeing our mysterious Marcos. By the way," I added in an attempt to lighten the conversation, "did you know you have an admirer?"

"A what!"

"An admirer," I repeated.

" 'Ere, what's all this, now?"

"There's a man sitting over there in the corner," I informed her with a conspiratorial wink, "who's been eyeing you ever since we sat down."

"What man?" was the flustered reply.

"Don't turn around! Wait 'til he's not looking—now!"

She turned her head in an affected casual manner in the direction of my eyes. "What, him!" she announced, taking in the measure of the man in the process of wiping beer froth from his mouth with the aid of a worn cuff. "He's been looking at me? Whatever for, I wonder?"

"As I say, perhaps he fancies you," I teased.

"Right!" was the contemptuous reply.

"Good Lord!"

"What?"

"He's coming over."

He approached with cap in hand as would a schoolboy seeking an audience with the headmaster. As to his age, I could only guess. Early forties or, perhaps, early fifties. It's difficult to determine the age of those who labor on the docks or at sea; time takes a heavy toll on both face and body. I would add that, beneath a shock of shaggy white hair with hanging forelock, two slightly puffed mischievous eyes were set betwixt a small, upturned, red-veined nose. Add to that the ill-fitting coat with all but one of its buttons missing, the green neckerchief that could have used a good washing, coupled with baggy trousers riding two inches above the ankles, and you have a summation of the man who stood before us. For some strange reason, he reminded me of an elf. One other thing I should mention. Incredible as it may seem, the man exuded a strong scent of cinnamon. It seemed to emanate from every pore.

"Good day to you, ladies," he addressed us, in a light Irish lilt. Not an elf, I thought, a leprechaun. We acknowledged the greeting with a silent nodding of heads.

"Beggin' your pardon, missus," he went on, directing his attention to Vi, who eyed him in wary apprehension, "but ever since you came in, there was meself sittin' over there thinkin' that we've met somewhere before."

"Oh, aye?" was the quick retort. "And where was that, then? Ascot?"

"Faith, now!" he laughed. "It *is* you. There'd be no mistaking that voice and sharp tongue. It's Mrs. Warner, it is. Mrs. Verna Warner, or I'm not who I think I am."

"It's Violet. Violet Warner," she corrected him, speaking very slowly with eyes that searched that puffy face for recognition.

"Violet Warner, it is, to be sure," was the lighthearted reply. "You'll be forgivin' me, I know, but it's been that many years."

"Has it now?" she queried. "And just who is it that you think you are?"

"Would you not be knowin'?" he responded, stepping back to allow full measure to be taken of his five-foot-five frame, " 'Tis Paddy," he announced, with a widening smile. "Paddy O'Ryan, himself."

"Paddy O'Ryan," repeated Vi, while questioning eyes continued to scan the face. "Why, so it is!" she at last exclaimed. Then, turning excitedly to me, she added, "You wouldn't know, Em, but Paddy here worked for my Bert at the chandlery after your William passed away and you moved on."

"Well, then." I smiled. "Pull up a chair and join us, Mr. O'Ryan."

"Thank you, ma'am, I'll do just that. And it's Paddy, it is, Mrs. Hudson, to all who know me," he added, after introductions and a set of drinks had been passed around.

"Fancy, Em and I were just talkin' 'bout the old days and the chandlery, and then you pop up out of nowhere. Is it still there?"

"The chandlery?"

"Aye."

"Not for more years than I care to remember. From what I'd be knowin' of it, the old fellow who bought it from you couldn't make a go of it. I'd not be knowin' what's there now."

"Well, then," pressed Vi, "what have you been doin' with yourself since then, eh?"

"Anything at all to keep body and soul together," he confessed. "Took to the sea for a spell before these old legs got too old for climbing the rigging. After that"—he shrugged—"this and that, Mrs. Warner, this and that."

"Pardon my asking, Mr. O'Ryan—Paddy," I corrected myself, "but I seem to detect the aroma of cinnamon."

"Ah, do you now?" He laughed. "I shouldn't wonder. 'Tis the sweet scent of No. 6 you'd be smellin'."

"No. 6?"

"No. 6 Warehouse," he stated. "I get odd jobs down there from time to time loading bales of cinnamon."

"And you can't wash it off?"

"Wash?"

The startled look we received, coupled with his reply, evoked a hidden smile twixt Vi and myself before I put forward the following question: "Then, I take it, you continue to live and work down here?"

"Aye, these twenty years and more."

"Then, perhaps," I continued, once more removing the picture from my purse, "you've seen this gentleman in here?"

"And who might he be then?" he asked, taking picture in hand.

"Well, it's no use tellin' him he's your brother, or mine either, for that matter," was Violet's pronouncement from across the table.

I agreed. Despite his fey manner, I was of the opinion that Paddy O'Ryan was nobody's fool.

I gambled on taking him into our confidence, at least to a certain extent. "Mrs. Warner and I," I confided, "have been asked by a certain gentleman to locate the man whose picture you now hold. That being said, my question is, have you ever seen this man in here, say, within the last month?"

"In Shandling's?"

"Yes."

" 'Tis truly sorry, I am, ladies," he announced after a pause, "but I'd be lyin' if I said I had. But what would this be now, about your brother?" he added, handing the sketch back to me.

"Aye, well, the thing of it is," confessed Violet, "we've been tellin' everybody that we've been looking for our long-lost brother, like."

"Faith, now!" An impish grin eased its way into that leathery, weather-beaten face. "You'd be gettin' just as far with that story as trying to catch the wind with furled sails."

"Oh, aye? And what's that supposed to mean?" snapped Violet, feeling a little foolish and not knowing exactly why.

"Why," he announced, "they probably figured he was your husband, don't you see? No man would be after spilling the whereabouts of another to a wife. Gentleman's agreement, you might say," he knowingly confided.

"Gentleman's agreement!" snapped Vi, with an indignant sneer.

"Then I'm afraid it's all been for nothing." I sighed, buttoning my gloves as we rose to take our leave.

"Aye," agreed my companion in similar de-

spondent tone. "It's been nowt more than a vin-
egar trip, this has, and no mistake."

"I could tell you where he'd be livin' if that
would be any help to you," announced Paddy
in a casual manner, before draining the last remains of his drink.

We dropped back into our chairs, stunned.
"You know where he lives? You've seen him?"

"Why didn't you say that in the first place?"
was Violet's angry contribution to my questions.

It seemed perfectly obvious to Paddy. "And
wasn't it you, Mrs. Hudson, who asked if I'd
seen him in here?" he asked, seemingly of-
fended by Violet's tirade. "And wasn't it me
who told you that I hadn't? But," he went on,
"where he lives, now that would be another
matter altogether."

"Flamin' Nora!" exclaimed Vi. "If you
aren't—"

"Paddy's perfectly right, Violet," I grudgingly interjected. "At least," I added, to save
face, "in a literal sense, that is."

"Well, what's the address, then?" demanded
my companion.

"Ah, well, you see, the funny thing of it is,"
he answered in a serious vein, or as serious as
that pug-nosed face could be, "I'm sometimes
gettin' what you might call a memory loss from
time to time."

"And what," I smiled, in anticipation of his
answer, "is the cause of this memory loss of
yours?"

"The doctors tell me it's from a lack of whiskey," he piously informed us. "You wouldn't

believe how a good shot of foin whiskey sets
the memory wheels spinning round faster than
an Irish jig."

Violet threw up her hands in hopeless frustration.

I ordered a double from "ducks," which our
little leprechaun downed in one gulp.

"It's all coming back to you now, is it?" was
Violet's caustic comment, as the empty glass
was returned to the table.

"As clear as the lakes of Killarney," he announced with a smile and a belch before adding, "Tench Street."

"Tenth, did you say?"

"Tench," he corrected me. "He's got himself
lodgings over on Tench Street."

"Do you know where?"

"I could take you there."

" 'Ere, now," announced Vi, eyeing him with
no little suspicion, "are you sure of what you're
telling us?"

"Am I sure, she says!" was the indignant reply. "And wasn't it me who got the toe of his
boot in me back no more than two days ago?"

"What's this?" I asked.

"It was late at night, Mrs. Hudson," he informed me, "while I was takin' a wee bit of a
rest, you might say, on the bottom stoop,
when—"

" 'A wee bit of a rest,' he says," interjected
my companion in a typical aside. "Passed out
would be more like it."

"Ah, Mrs. Warner," sighed he, " 'tis a cruel
woman, you are."

"Go, on, Paddy," I urged.

"So, there was meself, as I say, on the bottom stoop of the lodging house . . ."

"The one on Tench?"

"The very same. When all of a sudden I feel this kick in me backside. I looks up to see towering over me, himself, as in the picture, shaking his fist and bellowing out in a queer sort of accent for me to be on my way."

"You're sure it was the same man?" I pressed, knowing Paddy to be in his cups at the time.

"I'd not be forgettin' that face, Mrs. Hudson," he solemnly confirmed. "Or his hands."

"His hands?"

"I could tell as soon as I saw them," he went on, "that he wasn't from around here. Quite the gentleman's hands they were. Ten fingers that never saw a good day's work between the lot of them. And that's the truth of it."

I was positively elated at what we had heard, as was Violet. Here was proof, if Paddy was to be believed, and I saw no reason why he shouldn't be, that our quarry was indeed not only in England, but no more than a few streets away at best. The question was—could he be here on this side of the Channel, as Mr. Churchill had stated, "simply cooling his heels," or, turning the other side of the Churchillian coin over, could his presence denote that a bombing or assassination loomed in the offing?

In any event, it was evident to me that two women engaged in a surveillance amid the seamier sections of the waterfront would best be served, as to our safety, with the presence of a man, even if that man was a five-foot-five little gnome of a fellow named Paddy O'Ryan.

Happily, he agreed to my request that he serve as a companion in crime detection with us, my only stipulation being that his fee would be paid once we were over and done with it. I had no wish to be continually supplying him with money for "foin" Irish whiskey. If he was to be the third party to a triumvirate, I wanted him sober. It was also agreed we would all meet outside the Shandling House at seven o'clock that very night and, in the meantime, Paddy was to make an effort to secure a room for us, if that was possible, on the opposite side of the street where Marcos was lodged. That taken care of, Violet and I departed back to Baker Street in order to prepare supper. Needless to say, the menu would not consist of meat pies.

THREE

Off to War

⇛WHEN WE HAD MET as agreed outside Shandling's, we were informed by Paddy he was unable to locate a room we might rent in order to proceed with our surveillance. However, there was, he told us, a vacated store directly across the street from the house that lodged Marcos, with living quarters above it as empty as the shop itself. We congratulated ourselves on our good fortune and, upon our arrival, made our way down a narrow alley to the back of the shop and proceeded up a set of rickety steps to the landing. One might properly ascertain the extent of that rotted staircase when, with Violet bringing up the rear, our weight eventually caused a step to snap in the middle. A cry from Vi, whose foot was now caught fast, coupled with the sound of cracking wood, was enough to set a dog a-barking from somewhere within that dark patch of night. When Violet had extracted her foot and found she had been more frightened than hurt, we paused on the landing and waited in silence. With the barking now having ceased, and no one having ventured out to investigate the disturbance, we entered through the back door and, lighting a candle, gingerly made our way across the room.

"Well, I don't see how much this is going to help," muttered Vi, taking a hefty swipe with a rag as grimy as the window she was now attempting to clean.

"Let me be doin' that for you, Mrs. Warner," offered Paddy, while placing in front of the window the second of two chairs he had found, along with the rag, within the darkened recess of the room.

"No need," announced Vi, discarding the rag and taking her place beside me while Paddy seated himself on an empty wooden crate to our left. "It's as good as it's going to get. Did you bring just the one candle?" she asked of me, taking note of the flickering flame's struggle to shed what little light it could in that draught-bedeviled room.

"One should be enough," I answered. "We don't want to call attention to ourselves by having the place lit up like a Christmas tree."

Across the street a light shone forth from the second-floor window wherein lodged our mysterious Mr. M. If it had been daylight, if there had been no fog drifting in and out like some spectral being, and if our window had been properly cleaned, I daresay we would have had a perfect sighting. However, all was not lost.

"Why, Emma Hudson," quizzed my companion, as I withdrew a pair of field glasses from my bag, "wherever did you get those?"

"Actually," I confessed, "they're Dr. Watson's."

"Oh, aye?" she announced with a saucy wink. "Nipped them from the good doctor then, did you?"

"Certainly not!" I declared. "I simply borrowed them, you might say. After all," I added in defensive tone, "as far as I know, he hasn't used them since seeing service in Afghanistan. Besides," I went on, hoping to put an end to the matter, "I made use of them during the Haddley affair, and he was none the wiser."

"There'd be someone at the window, now, Mrs. Hudson!" the little man beside us suddenly sang out.

"Quick, Paddy," I cried, thrusting the glasses at him, "tell me if it's the same man the toe of whose boot you're so familiar with."

After a few minor adjustments to the lens, he announced that although he couldn't get a clear sighting owing to the hazards as previously stated, it was enough to enable him to respond in the affirmative.

"Right, then," I announced, flicking open the silver lid casing on my locket watch. "It's eight o'clock now; we'll stay 'til either he goes out, in which case we will proceed to follow him, or, if he remains inside, we'll call a halt at midnight."

"Midnight?" echoed Paddy. "That'd be four hours from now. Would you be havin'—"

"Mrs. Warner," I informed him, "has brought along a bottle of wine and a few cheese sandwiches."

"Wine?" was the crestfallen reply.

" 'Ere, now," announced an indignant Violet. "I'm not running a ruddy pub for the likes of you, Paddy O'Ryan! If wine's not to your liking—"

"Ah, Mrs. Warner," was the now ingratiating reply, "I'd not be one for refusin' any drink from a bottle. And it's a charmin' woman, you are, for thinkin' of bringing it along."

That being said, we settled down and waited. At eleven o'clock the light from the window across the street went out. Was he about to depart? After another hour with no Marcos descending the outside steps, it was evident he had turned in for the night. We then left at our designated hour, after agreeing to return at seven the following evening.

And so it was that we arrived back on Sunday night to resume our vigil. Noticing that as the evening wore on, Violet's eyelids began drooping in rhythm with her head, I suggested we spell ourselves at hourly intervals. As for myself, I was thankful I had set time aside earlier in the day for an afternoon nap. And while the wooden chairs, the only pieces of furniture in that otherwise barren room, were not the most comfortable in the world, in retrospect, it was probably just as well, as it would have been too easy to drift off had we access to a cushioned chesterfield or leathered chair. Even so, I must admit I was growing somewhat weary.

As for Paddy, who for the most part helped in whiling away the hours by quietly singing (lest he be heard by some passing patrolman) bawdy ballads and folk songs in a surprisingly

pleasant, light Irish tenor, he had himself now
fallen silent. Surrounded as we were in a room
of candlelight and shadows, it was difficult to
see whether he was asleep or not. No matter,
thought I, stifling a yawn. It would be only another twenty minutes or so before I'd be nudg-
ing Violet to take over the watch. However, I
was soon jolted out of my lethargy by the
sound of hoofbeats coming to a stop on the
street below.

In my haste in leaning forward toward the
window, I accidentally knocked over the field
glasses I had previously placed on the floor beside my chair. The thud of it startled a groggy
Violet into waking. "What is it?" she asked,
with a light rubbing of the eyes. "What's happened?"

"A horse!" I cried, while in the process of
retrieving the glasses.

"A horse?" was Paddy's drowsy response.
"Where?"

"Well, it's not in the room, is it!" snapped a
now fully awakened Violet.

"There's someone getting out of the cab that's
just pulled up," I excitedly informed them,
while continuing to focus in on the scene below.
"From what I can make out," I continued, "he
seems to be a well-tailored individual."

"Ah, well, then, he wouldn't be from around
here. 'Cept maybe he's the landlord."

"I think not, Paddy." I smiled. "Not at this
time of night. Someone's just opened the door.
I can't see who." A pause. "He's talking to the
man who just arrived." Another pause.
"They're inside now. The door's been closed."

With that, I sank back into my chair.

"You know, Em," announced Violet, "I'm not one to put a damper on things, but there's nowt to say it was Marcos he was calling on. Could have been anybody in a lodging house, it could."

"We'll soon see. Keep an eye on the upstairs window, will you?" I asked, handing over the glasses. "If I'm right, we should soon see two men inside that room."

After no more than a minute or so, which in truth seemed like twenty, Vi suddenly announced: "You're right, Em. There *are* two men in there!"

"Could I be takin' a look, Mrs. Warner?" asked Paddy.

As our new compatriot took his post at the window, I remarked to Vi that now, at least, we had some measure of information to pass along to Mr. Churchill, who, while not contacting me on Friday last as I had expected, would no doubt be in touch before the new week was out. Unless this was but one of his many irons in the fire he would eventually leave to sizzle out. However, I thought that most unlikely. Mr. Churchill, if I had judged him correctly, had the tenacity of a bulldog and would see this, or any other commitment that might command his attention, through to its final conclusion. As to just what that final conclusion would be, only time would tell.

"Would you look at that, now," remarked Paddy, to no one in particular.

"What is it? What do you see?" asked Vi.

"Seems they'd be havin' a bit of a set-to, you

might say," he answered from the window.

"Here, let me have a look," I said, taking my place beside him as he relinquished the glasses. "Yes, you're right," I concurred, trying to get as sharp a focus as possible through one grimy window over to the other across the street that, no doubt, was equally in need of a good washing. "I can make out one of them waving his arms about as if engaged in some sort of a heated discussion," I added to both Vi and Paddy, who had now taken a stance on either side of me. "Look out!" I suddenly called out, on noting that one of the men had come full face to the window. We jumped back and waited until, with curiosity getting the better of us, we peeked round the window frame like three naughty children. "He's looking around," I whispered. Though why in a whisper, I don't know, other than it seemed apropos to the situation.

"Did he see us?" asked Violet.

"No, I don't think so," I answered, as the face disappeared behind a now drawn curtain.

We ended our watch shortly after midnight, when our well-tailored gentleman at last took his departure. Pausing momentarily as he did, after descending the three steps that led from the lodging house onto the street, I had hoped to use that moment to distinguish and remember his features. However, pale yellow orbs of light from gaslit lamps threw little light on my subject, so that he remained but a shadowy figure who within moments had disappeared into a vapored mist. To follow him would have been impossible. We took our leave.

*   *   *

"Would you care for anything while you're waiting, madam?" asked the hawk-nosed waiter of regal presence who had suddenly materialized as if out of nowhere at my elbow.

"Thank you, no," I replied, managing a wan smile and feeling a trifle intimidated by his "to the manner born" demeanor. I received a slight bow of the head in acknowledgment as he silently withdrew across a rose-patterned weave of plush carpeting.

Little did I realize when awakening Monday morning that the afternoon would find me in a posh dining room awaiting young Mr. Churchill's arrival. It had been shortly after one o'clock when Violet had entered the parlor to inform me a note from that gentleman had just arrived by messenger. In haste I tore open the envelope and read to my companion, who was as eager as I to know its content, that it was our client's wish I meet with him at four o'clock that very afternoon for tea at Simpson's.

So, there I sat in ruffled blouse of white with bow of color corresponding to my navy blue tailor-made suit and velvet toque with its spray of egret feathers (hastily sewn back on before departing) set at a just-so angle atop my head, feeling very elegant, indeed.

The room was a study in quiet grandeur, with the sound of silver-plated cutlery and bone china plates, from the clearing of tables, being the only audible distraction to the murmur of conversation from the adjoining tables. Although melodious music in a minor key, provided by a string quartet hidden behind the obligatory vases of ferns and palms, added a dignified tone to the overall ambience of the room, I would have preferred to have heard something a little more lively. Other than that, and the fact that I would have gladly exchanged my waiter for dear old "ducks" at Shandling's, I was completely enchanted with my surroundings.

Continuing in my wait for Mr. Churchill, I unbuttoned my pearl-gray gloves, laying one atop the other on the white linen tablecloth, and casually draped my Inverness over the back of the chair. It was, as I recall, light mauve in color, and I remember feeling very daring when first purchasing the coat, black having been up to that time the predominant color of my attire. Come along, then, Mr. Churchill. I smiled to myself. "Lady" Hudson awaits. As if in response to my command, the gentleman himself suddenly appeared at the entrance of the foyer, and, after a word or two with the maître d', who I observed nodding in my direction, he approached with purposeful stride to greet me.

"Ah, Mrs. Hudson, how charming you look," was the gracious response I received on his approach to the table. "Dreadfully sorry I'm late," he added apologetically, while taking a seat opposite. "Couldn't be helped, I'm afraid."

"Perfectly alright. Think nothing of it, Mr. Churchill," I gushed in Grand Lady-like manner, with an airy wave of my hand and, in the process, came within a hairbreadth of overturning the glass of water placed to my right. Grand Lady indeed, I moaned inwardly. Mutton dressed as lamb, would be more like it. Just be yourself, Emma Hudson, I told myself. There's no one else who can play the part better.

"I've ordered tea," he announced, thankfully with no mention or notice of my near mishap. "They serve it here along with flaky pastry shells filled with strawberry jam," he confided, as would a child revealing some wonderful secret. "Simply delicious, my dear Mrs. Hudson." He beamed. "Simply delicious. Now then," he continued in a more businesslike mood, "what have you found out? If nothing, I shan't be too surprised." On seeing my somewhat hurt and startled reaction to what I perceived as an ungallant remark, he quickly added, "Oh, no, you misunderstand me. I meant no reflection on your capabilities, madam. It's just, what with the war dragging on and all, I'm afraid the Yard is seeing assassins behind every lamppost."

Scotland Yard now, is it? thought I. How smoothly the transition from originator to bystander is shifted. "Then, no doubt, Mr. Churchill," I announced a trifle smugly, "you'll be surprised to hear—" I stopped as a tea service was set before us.

"There, what did I tell you!" he exclaimed, feasting his eyes on the strawberry turnovers. "Fit for a king, wouldn't you say?"

"Indeed," I agreed. "Perhaps, even for a future prime minister?"

"Haw!" he chortled aloud with a slap to the table and, in so doing, brought steely-eyed stares of disapproval from the surrounding patrons. "Are you a fortune-teller as well as a detective, madam?" he cried out in good-humored fashion, unaware of the minor disturbance he was causing.

"Are you as an ambitious a man as I think you are?" I answered back.

"By Jove! I like you, Mrs. Hudson. I really do!" he roared in delight (causing more clucking of tongues from nearby tables). "Now, what's all this about my being surprised?" he asked, while methodically licking a spot of jam off the tip of his thumb.

"I have found the gentleman in question," I quietly informed him, with a touch of pride in my voice.

His mouth dropped open in utter amazement, and, for the first time since seating himself at the table, he was momentarily speechless. "Marcos?" he at last blurted out. "Here? Where? In London?"

"He has lodgings on Tench Street near the London Dock," I answered, suppressing a smile at the almost comical look on his face as he sought to come to grips with this unexpected turn of events. Tea and turnovers were forgotten as he fumbled about in an agitated manner before at last extracting a cigar. "You've actually seen him?" he queried, as a match was struck in conjunction with the question.

"Yes," I answered simply.

At that, he leaned thoughtfully back in his chair, studying me quietly for a moment or two as wisps of smoke lazily wafted their way upward into nothingness. "Tell me about it," he said at last, when, in truth, what he meant was "prove it to me."

I was ready for him.

I began by informing him of the various inquiries conducted over the past week by both Mrs. Warner and myself, of our chance meeting with Mr. O'Ryan, resulting in our subsequent vigil of the Tench Street lodging, and of our quarry's mysterious midnight caller. I spoke extemporaneously, referring only from time to time to my note pad for dates, times, and places.

"Excellent, Mrs. Hudson." He beamed in approval when I had finished. "Quite thorough, quite professional. I *am* pleased. You see," he added with a wave of his cigar, "what does the Yard know, eh? With Marcos here, something's afoot, madam. Mark my words."

"Perhaps. Perhaps, not," I stated honestly. "Whether he's up to no good or not, we have, at this point in time, no way of knowing."

"True, true," he mused. "But what about Marcos and this 'midnight caller' chap?" he inquired of me. "They were seen to be arguing, you say?"

"Yes, but as to the nature of the argument I can only guess."

"And that guess would be?" he asked, leaning forward in his chair.

"It has been my understanding," I began, "that when two men have a falling-out it's usually for one of two reasons. Women or money. In this particular case, I think we're safe in assuming it was money."

"The beggar's upped the ante," he announced thoughtfully. "That would be my guess."

"Ah, to have had Vi in that room," I said, voicing my thoughts aloud.

"What's that you say?" was the puzzled response from across the table. "—to have had *Vi* in that room? I don't—"

Oh, dear, now I've done it. Think fast. Emma, I told myself. "You misunderstand me," I answered in lighthearted fashion. "I said, ah, to have been a *fly* in that room." Not bad, old girl.

"A fly?" he persisted.

"A saying, Mr. Churchill," I smiled. "Nothing more."

I, of course, had been referring to Vi's secret astral capabilities of releasing her spiritual self from her physical body. Although her powers in these out-of-body experiences had proved exceedingly helpful during our investigation of the Haddley Hall murders, I had no intention of requesting similar "astral journeys" of her. While I had no compunction about using whatever means available, the return of spirit to body was ofttimes a traumatic experience for her; that, coupled with her age, was the overriding factor in my decision.

"Dash it all," my table companion suddenly blurted out. "I've been so engrossed in all this Marcos business, I completely forgot to tell you *my* news!"

"Your news?" I responded with casual interest as I set about the refilling of my cup. "What news would that be, Mr. Churchill?"

"I'm off to war, madam!" he announced triumphantly.

"War!" I blurted out, a little too loudly I'm afraid, whereupon it was I who was now the recipient of hostile glances from within the room, including those of our imperious waiter.

"The, ah, tablecloth, Mrs. Hudson."

"The what?"

"It seems you've poured your tea on the tablecloth," he delicately informed me, indicating a stain seeping its way across the linen.

"Whatever must you think?" I asked, feeling the fool at having so utterly embarrassed myself.

"I think it looks like Africa," he answered.

"Like what?"

"Africa," he repeated, pointing to the stain, now enlarged by half. "See, it resembles the coastline of Africa. Do you think it could be a sign?" he asked in all earnestness.

He completely bewildered me. "I'm afraid I don't understand," I answered.

"As I say, I'm off to war—South Africa, Mrs. Hudson. Perhaps this," he announced, indicating the stained tablecloth, "is a sign of great things to come. Or else," he added, his face suddenly clouding over in thought, "it's a portent of—"

"Perhaps it's a sign unto you not to drink the tea," I chuckled, in an attempt to lighten his mood. "But, tell me," I asked, while quickly laying napkin over stain lest our waiter should chance upon it, "what's all this about you going off to war?"

The face broke out into a boyish grin as he began by announcing that in two days hence he'd be sailing aboard the *Dunottar Castle* for Natal, South Africa, to cover the Boer uprising as war correspondent for the *Morning Post*. Af-

ter my initial reaction of astonishment at this
unexpected turn of events, he went on to regale
me with tales of his past exploits as a military
journalist in both Cuba and India, as well of his
adventures the year previous with Kitchener's
Army of the Sudan.

What a fascinating man, I thought. I had
never met his like before. Yet, even as he spoke,
I couldn't help but wonder if this latest venture
of his would signal the end of the Marcos investigation. Sailing off, as he was, to a continent
an ocean away, it hardly seemed likely there
would be a need for a continuation of my services. And I said as much.

"Why, of course I want you to continue on,
my dear Mrs. Hudson," he exclaimed in surprise. "There was never any doubt that you
should."

"But, with you in South Africa—"

"There's no need to trouble yourself on that
score." He smiled knowingly. "Everything's
been arranged. There's a young chap I know at
the *Post*, name's Henten. Miles Henten," he
continued, "whom I've taken into my confidence with regard to Marcos and your investigation. You'll report to him while I'm away.
However," he added, withdrawing a small
crumpled sheet of paper from his waistcoat,
"should you have a need to contact me, I've
written down an address where I can be
reached in Natal."

I nodded in understanding as I slipped the
paper into my purse. "Henten, you say?" I
asked, once more bringing forth my note pad.

"Yes, Miles Henten. Awfully decent chap.

You'll like him. I've arranged for you to meet him at the *Post* on the eleventh if that's convenient."

"Yes, of course," I answered, adding, "The eleventh, your day of sailing?"

"Yes, it is, actually," he acknowledged. "Terribly sorry to miss the meeting and all that, but," he added with a mischievous wink, "it wouldn't do to keep the Boers waiting, now would it?"

FOUR

All Around the Town

∞AS THE HANSOM clip-clopped its way through the bustling, sun-dappled streets of London, I couldn't help but marvel at what a glorious morning it had turned out to be. A rare and wonderful change for an October day whose like, no doubt, would not be seen again for many a month to come. Indeed, the sun seemed fairly bursting with pride as it spread its warmth over a street filled with Londoners busily going to and fro about their business. As was I. Having never seen the inside workings of a newspaper office before, I was quite looking forward to my meeting with Mr. Henten.

On approaching my destination, horse and cabby found themselves not only caught up in a stream of congested traffic but, with carriages of every size and description lining the curb on either side of the street, were afforded little or no space in which to rein up. As it was fast approaching the hour of my appointment, I paid my fare and, alighting from the cab, took my chances in and around the onrush of neighing and snorting horses, accompanied in turn by the cries and bellows of their drivers, before at last reaching the sanctity and safety of the pavement. As I paused momentarily to catch my breath, I saw I was no more than a door down from the *Morning Post* itself. It was at that point I noticed a gentleman, who had just exited that establishment, advancing in lengthy strides toward me.

A tall, well-built man, close to six feet, I should imagine, with an air of authority which he wore as easily as he did the single-breasted, three-piece gabardine suit. Being hatless, as he was, I could see his sandy blond hair, with just the slightest wave to it, was neatly trimmed while his clear blue eyes, of which I took note on his approach, curiously enough emitted no more emotion than would two beacons of light. As to his age, I should say somewhere in his late thirties. All in all, a quite handsome gentleman who would cause many a maiden to flutter her fan, if, indeed, maidens still fluttered fans.

"You must be Mrs. Hudson," he said with accompanying smile. "I'm Henten, Miles Henten," he added, with the smile disappearing in tandem with the introduction.

"Oh," I replied, momentarily taken aback, having thought I'd be meeting a much younger man. I acknowledged his greeting, though a trifle flustered by this on-the-street introduction, by adding, "You needn't have come out to meet me. I was just—"

"Yes, well, the thing of it is," he broke in, "it looks as if we won't be able to keep our meeting after all, I'm afraid." He went hurriedly on to explain that his managing editor had unexpectedly called a staff meeting for eleven o'clock that very morning, and, as it was now fast approaching that hour, he could spare me but a few minutes at best. I was, of course, upset at this bit of news but, I told myself, such are the ways of the workaday world.

"I say, are you really a detective?" he asked, eyeing me up and down as if I were an item in a display case. "I could do a piece on you, if you like."

"A piece?"

"An article," he explained. "In the paper. London's first official female detective, and all that," he added in a thinly disguised, thin-lipped smirk.

Was I to take him seriously? Perhaps the question would best be served by turning it around: was *he* taking *me* seriously? In any event, I found him a little too glib for my liking. "Mr. Henten," I stated most unequivocally. "In the first place, I am not an 'official' anything, and, in the second place, I should like to make it perfectly clear that I seek no publicity for myself whatsoever. Now, as to the matter at hand," I continued, in like manner, "I take it Mr. Churchill has brought you up-to-date on my findings in regard to the Marcos investigation?"

"Your findings?" That seemed to set him aback. "Why, no," he added, a trifle flustered. "I've not spoken to Mr. Churchill since being told of our meeting. He only pops into the office now and then," he went on, by way of explanation. "It's not as if he were a regular employee. Freelances, you know. Now the chap's taken himself off to South Africa, so you see . . ." There followed a hunch to the shoulders and an open spread of the hands in a gesture of futility.

"I can well appreciate your situation," I sympathized. "It does appear that our Mr. Churchill is quite the gadabout. But, be that as it may," I continued in an even tone, "I do have some information to pass along to you."

"What? Oh, yes . . . information." The words drifted off as his concentration shifted to two men waving to him in recognition as they descended from the newspaper office onto the street. As he returned the wave I noticed a large chunky signet ring on the third finger of his right hand. It immediately brought to mind my late husband, who could not abide a ringed finger on any man. As I recall, it was only after much cajoling on my part that he finally consented to wear a wedding ring, albeit grudgingly. Whether he thought such an affectation denoted a less than masculine quality or not, I have no idea. But I digress.

"Yes, you, ah, were saying something about information?" spoke the gentleman from the *Post*, now with a slight edginess to the voice and exhibiting an overall appearance of someone decidedly ill at ease. Strange, I thought. Why this sudden change in demeanor? Surely the reason wasn't due to his fellow employees who waved in recognition. I could only conclude at the time it was I, keeping him too long from his meeting. "I'll be brief," I stated. "Marcos is in London. I have his address here," I added, handing over a slip of paper.

"You know where he's lodged!" he gasped.

"Yes," I answered matter-of-factly. "I might also mention he had a visitor on Sunday night last. Although, I might add, I could not describe him in any detail owing to the poor visibility of the night."

"No matter, Mrs. Hudson. All in all, excellent work, I must say." And while the blue eyes smiled, the voice carried as much conviction to the words as would Paddy O'Ryan taking the pledge. I, or something, had upset him. It would appear I no longer represented a figure of fun for some forthcoming article. Did he believe in some way I would diminish his role in the Marcos affair? In essence, was he afraid the lady detective would steal the newspaperman's thunder? All this, of course, was nothing but conjecture on my part at the time, and I saw no reason in raising the issue with him.

After another obligatory word or two of congratulations, the promise to be in touch shortly, and the voicing of a hurried goodbye, he took off at a half run back into the redbricked edifice of the *Morning Post*.

Well, thought I, that was short and sweet. "A nice chap, you'll like him," Mr. Churchill had said. I didn't know if I did, really. Ah, well, to each his own.

It had been a good three weeks since that meeting with Miles Henten, though perhaps I should amend that. While it had been three weeks, they definitely were not good ones. No, frustrating would be the better word, for it had consisted for the most part in the trailing of Marcos. Exciting as that may appear to be to the armchair detective, in reality it was a footsore and wearisome exercise in futility.

I had put it to Violet and Paddy that if or when our quarry ventured out of his lair, we would each take turns in following him and report back with our findings as to where he went, what he saw, etc. What strange, mysterious, and foreboding places, we wondered, would he lead us to? Incredible as it may seem, we followed him not to sinister opium dens or secret meetings of international anarchists, nor, for that matter, to the man we had first seen enter his Tench Street lodgings, but to those sights of greater London as would be visited by the most ordinary of tourists.

On one particular day on which I had the dubious honor of "shadowing" him, as they say, he had taken himself to Trafalgar Square. And there we stood—I, eyeing Marcos; he, surveying Nelson atop his column, while the admiral, oblivious to us mortals down below, continued to maintain his never-ending one-eyed vigil over the London skyline. As I continued to keep Marcos under close observation as he aimlessly traipsed up and down the streets, engaged in nothing more clandestine than a bit of shopping or stopping off for a bite to eat, there was nothing at day's end to indicate that anything of a suspicious nature had taken place.

Other days might find me following him into the House of Commons where I would take a seat just to the back of him up in the visitors' gallery as our elected representatives on the floor below endlessly debated government policy, or the lack of it, in regard to the Boer War crisis. How we in Britain were faring in that ongoing conflict depended, it would seem, on which side of the aisle the honorable members sat. I remember being disappointed in missing the opportunity of being able to see the prime minister himself take part in those heated discussions; his ongoing absence, as stated by the deputy prime minister during the question period, was due to ill health.

With regard to Marcos I observed that he sat viewing the proceedings in stoic silence without giving the slightest indication whatsoever of interest. Whether this was due perhaps to a somewhat limited knowledge of the English language, I don't know. In any event, his visits were of a short duration. Not so those times he spent at the British Museum or the National Gallery. It was at the gallery, as I milled about with those strolling from room to room while being mindful to keep well to the back of him, that it became apparent to me as he stopped from time to time to admire a particular painting, be it a Gainsborough, Turner, Reynolds, or some equally skilled though lesser-known artist, that here was a man who had more of a passing interest in the world of art than ever he did for politics. How strange that someone who thought nothing of dispensing his fellow human beings into eternity for naught but the sake of profit could find beauty in the stroke of an artist's brush. As they say, it takes all kinds to make a world—and all kinds, it would seem, to destroy it.

As he continued to stand lost in thought before an early Holbein, I took advantage of noting that his face was not as brutish as had been portrayed in the charcoal sketch. No, this was not some slope-skulled Neanderthal as depicted by that artistic Belgian officer of the law who, in all likelihood, would have been more than a little biased toward his subject. While it was true the bushy eyebrows did lend a brooding appearance to the man, there was a certain intellectual demeanor about him; even the way he carried himself denoted a certain Continental flair. Had he been, I wondered, the wastrel son of a noble European family or a disgruntled professor dismissed from the fellowship for voicing political thoughts too radical for an august body of academicians—or simply an opportunist with little or no morals? Perhaps I would never know.

In any event, my sojourn through that veritable palace of paintings led me to think of my own undistinguished landscapes that hung not in galleries, but in what I laughingly referred to as the studio, in reality, the back porch leading off from my kitchen. With little room for an easel and not much else, including heat, it meant any attempt at putting oil to canvas was limited to the summer months only. As to the measure of my artistic abilities, I might mention that at one point Mr. Holmes offered to buy one of my seascapes. While delighted, I refused any payment and gave him the painting for his upstairs lodging. Having never again seen the picture from that day to this, I can only conclude the offer was made more out of pity than for any singular admiration that gentleman had of my talent. Still, I would not be discouraged, and I continued to paint whenever time, weather, and inclination coincided.

Speaking of Mr. Holmes, what, I wondered, would he have made of a situation in which a known terrorist, followed at every turn by either myself, Violet, or Mr. O'Ryan, strolls aimlessly about the city leaving no mysterious packages to be picked up on deserted park benches, secretly passes no notes to a confederate on the street, in Parliament, the British Museum, or the National Gallery, and engages in no whispered conversations with an unknown second party in any one of an endless array of sights throughout the greater London area. I daresay the master criminologist would have found it most puzzling.

As did I.

FIVE

Off Again, On Again

THERE WERE NO two ways about it, the house was definitely in need of a proper cleaning from top to bottom. What with a goodly portion of our time taken up in the ongoing investigation, I'm afraid our household chores had fallen far behind; indeed, Violet herself was at that very minute keeping watch at our Tench Street hideaway. So, in dust cap, apron, and with feather duster in hand, I surveyed my parlor and exhaled a weary sigh at the prospect that lay before me. Although the Oriental rug, faded yet still serviceable, as well as the green velour drapes with their gold-fringed tassels would have to wait 'til spring for a good paddling over the clothesline, the curtains could and should be taken down and washed and the furniture and picture frames given a good dusting. And my pride and joy, the lovely three-foot-high brass candlestand of intricate Indian design that my late husband, William, had brought back from one of his many voyages to the Near East, was in need of a right smart polishing.

Where to begin? Happily, I was given a respite before I had even begun by the ringing of the outside bell. No doubt, I thought, another client seeking the services of Mr. Holmes.

"Why, Mr. Henten!" I exclaimed on opening the door and seeing that blond blue-eyed giant of a man standing before me. "This is a surprise."

"Mrs. Hudson, how are you?" he responded in gentlemanly fashion. "I haven't come at an inconvenient time, have I?" he added in conjunction with a slightly whimsical smile.

Now, why was he—Good, heavens, I still had my cap on and feather duster in hand. I could feel my face redden. Perhaps Violet was right in stating, as she did from time to time, that I put too much emphasis on being Miss Prim and Proper. Still, would Mr. Sherlock Holmes be caught addressing a client in overalls and rubber boots?

"Inconvenient?" I echoed in response. "No, not at all. Come in, come in," I announced, managing a faint smile. "I'll just take the bowler and brolly, shall I?" While placing them on the hall coat rack, with his back slightly turned toward me as he set about slipping out of his topcoat, I quickly whisked off my cap and quietly dropped the duster to the floor, giving it a light kick into the corner. "Still raining out then, is it?" I asked, leading him into the parlor.

"Dribs and drabs, Mrs. Hudson," he answered, easing his six-foot frame into the oc-

casional chair set betwixt table and chesterfield.
"Dribs and drabs."

"Perhaps you'd care for something, Mr. Henten?" I asked, stuffing my cap behind a throw
cushion as I took my place opposite him. "A
cup of—"

"Thank you, no," he demurred, with a wave
of the hand. "I'm afraid I'm running behind
schedule, as it is. Perhaps you could bring me
up-to-date on the Marcos investigation."

Thorough, precise, and to the point, that's our
Mr. Henten.

"Well," I addressed him with a plaintive
sigh, "if no news is good news, then I have
good news for you."

"How'd you mean?"

"It would appear," I confessed, "that our
mysterious Mr. Marcos is nothing more than a
tourist, at least on this trip." He leaned forward
in his chair as if about to speak, but I continued.
"He's been under surveillance a good three
weeks now," I stated most emphatically, "and
in all that time he has done nothing that could
possibly be construed in any way as being il-
legal."

"You're positive of this?" he pressed.

"Mr. Henten," I assured him, "the man
spends his time taking in the sights of London—the British Museum, Parliament, the National Gallery, and what have you. I know," I
added with a light chuckle. "I've got the aching
feet to prove it."

"My sympathies, Mrs. Hudson," was the un-
emotional response. "It must have been a tiring
experience for you."

Such a serious man. "Yes," I added, "but an enlightening one."

"Nevertheless," he went on, "from what you have told me, there's hardly any point in continuing with the investigation, is there?"

He was right, of course. And I stated as much to him. It had all seemed so promising at first, but, I had to admit, there was little point in continuing to survey a man whose only crime had been attempting to light a cigarette in the museum's rotunda. At the end of our chat, which, I should say, lasted no more than fifteen minutes, I thought to ask: "You'll inform Scotland Yard?"

"Of?"

"His presence," I stated. "I should imagine they would want to contact various European governments in regard to extradition proceedings. In that respect," I added, "we have at least accomplished something."

"Yes, you're quite right," he agreed on rising. "I'll put a call in to them this morning."

"And I'll see to it that Mr. Churchill is sent a telegram informing him of our decision," I announced on escorting my visitor to the door.

"I can do that for you, if you like, Mrs. Hudson," he offered, adjusting the bowler with a light tap to the crown.

"Why, that's ever so nice of you, Mr. Henten." I smiled. "That would save me a bit of time."

On reaching the outside step he turned to address me one last time before taking his leave. "It would have been a fantastic story, would it not?"

"If it involved no loss of life," I answered.

The blue eyes focused thoughtfully on me for a moment or two before he stated, quite simply, "Good day to you, Mrs. Hudson."

" 'Ere, what's this you're saying? Give it up! Why, whatever for?" So spoke Violet on hearing of my decision to abandon the case. "Vi," I reasoned, resting my purse on the small wooden table that Paddy had managed to scrounge up from Lord only knows where, "we simply must be practical. There's been no crime. Nor," I went on, taking the chair opposite, cushioned now, as was the other, thanks to my companion's foresight in bringing two along from home, "does it appear that one is about to be committed."

"But he's up to no good, Em," she remonstrated. "I can feel it in me bones."

"As do I," I confessed.

"Well, then," she asked, "why don't we leave it up to Mr. Churchill, eh? Wire him, see what he—"

"Mr. Henten," I cut in, "has already stated this morning that he'll be sending off a telegram to Mr. Churchill announcing that the case is to be abandoned."

"Mr. Henten, is it!" she exploded in vitriolic tone. "And who's he when he's at home, eh? How do you know whether he will or won't? Trying to take over the case for himself, like as not, from what you've been telling me. Send Mr. Churchill a telegram yourself, luv, is what I say."

Before committing myself one way or the

other, I caught the sound of feet clomping up the outside stairs. "Someone's coming!" I cried out in alarm. "Quick, the candle."

"It's nowt but Paddy," Violet assured me. "I can tell by the way he thumps up the steps. For a little fellow," she added in exasperation, "he makes more noise than a room full of ruddy elephants."

"Where's he been?" I asked.

"We saw Marcos leave not more than a half hour before you showed up," she explained. "Paddy left to follow him."

"Yet Marcos himself hasn't returned," I said, with an eye toward the window. "I've been watching that front stoop ever since I arrived."

"Would that be yourself, Mrs. Hudson?" sang out the third member of our trio as he stood framed in shadow within the doorway.

After beckoning him in and requesting he keep his voice down to at least a conversational level, we were informed by our slightly tipsy friend that Marcos had taken himself down to the local pub and, from the look of it had, as Paddy put it, settled himself down for some serious drinking. How our little leprechaun managed to find the money to wet his own whistle, I have no idea; nor did I ask. But, with Marcos now at the pub, it did, in truth, give me an idea.

"I think you should know, Paddy," I stated, "that Mrs. Warner and I have been talking about abandoning the case."

"Abandoning, you say!" was the surprised response as he sought relief from wobbly legs by steadying himself against the windowsill. "It's that sorry I am to hear it." Then, in a

change of mood, a knowing smile spread itself
across the stubbled face. "Ah, I see, come down
here yourself to be giving ol' Paddy what's owing him, have you? And isn't it about time,
too," he added with a gleeful rubbing of hands.
"What with me without so much as tuppence
to me name. And that's the truth of it, dear
lady."

"I'm afraid," I smiled, "you'll have to wait a
while yet for your 'pot of gold,' Mr. O'Ryan."

"What's this you're sayin', then?"

"I said," I reiterated, "that we were talking
about calling it off. I didn't say we were."

"Why, Emma Hudson," declared a thor-
oughly confused Violet, "I distinctly remember
you saying—"

"Yes, I know," I confessed, rising from the
chair to begin a thoughtful pacing over creaking
floorboards. "Still, I would like to have one last
go at it." It annoyed me to leave it hanging in
midair, so to speak. It needed one last gesture
or effort on my part before I'd be satisfied that
we had done all that we could and had gone as
far as we could go. "Paddy," I announced,
"you say Marcos has taken himself down to the
local and could remain there for an indefinite
period?" The little man nodded in assent.
"Right," I continued, with another glance out
the window. "Then we'll use that time in taking
ourselves over to his lodgings for a little look-
see, shall we?"

"His room?" queried Vi. "Whatever for?"

"Whatever for? That's just it, Violet," I answered with a bemused smile. "I haven't a
clue—literally. But it's something we should

have done before now. And," I went on, "if there's something there, anything, that will implicate Marcos in any way as to our suspicions, then it goes without saying that our investigation is still on."

"And if there be nothing there?" asked our Irish friend.

"Then, Paddy O'Ryan," I stated, "you'll be paid in full, and we can all go home to a good night's rest."

"But how will we ever get into his room?" questioned Vi.

"Ol' Paddy may be of some service to you there, ladies," announced the little fellow with a conspiratorial wink. Then, noting an arched eyebrow from yours truly, quickly added: "And it's a grand thing, it is, Mrs. Hudson, knowing I have the gift, you might say, for unlocking doors for poor unfortunate creatures who've lost their keys."

"Enough of your blarney, Paddy O'Ryan," snapped Vi. "Can you pick a lock, or not?"

"I can, that," he stated proudly.

After descending the back stairs, we waited in the shadows between alley and street until all was clear of aimless strollers before attempting to make our way over. Thankfully enough, we found on arriving that the front door had been left unlocked. Pausing for a moment or two within the vestibule to let our eyes become accustomed to the dark, we heard, from somewhere within those rented rooms, the angry voices of a male and female engaged in a heated argument. Would they arouse the inhabitants?

Would doors suddenly be flung open? We held our breath and waited. Surprisingly, it ended as quickly as it had erupted, not in a whimper but in a peal of laughter. As silence once more descended over us, we tiptoed our way up the staircase to the first-floor landing and down a dark, dank, garbage-infested hallway until arriving at the door in question. At which point Mr. O'Ryan withdrew some sort of wire from his pocket and proceeded to jiggle the inside mechanism of the lock while Vi and I waited anxiously behind him. Paddy was as good as his word. In less time than it takes to tell, the door swung silently open and we, just as silently, entered.

"Did you think to bring a candle?" I asked Vi from within the blackness of the room.

"Aye, candle and holder," she answered. "All I need now is a match. Paddy," she called out softly, "do you have a match on you?"

"I do," he answered. "But where are you?"

"Stay where you are," she advised, "I'll come to you."

"Is it cat's eyes you have, Mrs. Warner?" asked our cinnamon-scented friend.

"No," she answered, suppressing a giggle, "a woman's nose."

The light from the candle proved more than adequate within the small confines of the room. And, in the unlikely event Marcos should unexpectedly return, I placed Paddy at the window to stand watch. As for the room itself, it was utilitarian at best. A single bed, with a dangerously low sag in its middle, was pushed up alongside a scarred and marred three-drawer dresser, on whose cigarette-burned top rested a chipped porcelan bowl and pitcher. At right angles to the pitcher a once well-thumbed Bible lay gathering dust while, ironically enough, a small circular glass ashtray to its left sat spotlessly clean. The drawers revealed nothing more than a few toilet items, a towel, two shirts, one or two cravats, and underwear. Though, I might add, all carefully folded and/or neatly arranged. Inside the boxlike cupboard hung one suit, a pair of shoes, and an umbrella. A leather-strapped suitcase and a Gladstone bag (both empty) were found under the bed.

"Travels light, don't he?" observed Vi with a wry smile.

"Have you found out nothin', then?" asked our window-bound sentry.

"Not a flamin' thing, from what I can see," answered my companion in a weary tone.

"Nothing, you say, Mrs. Warner?" I retorted, a trifle too smugly I'm afraid.

She turned toward me and, as she did so, the flickering light set her profile in silhouette. With her head turned slightly at a questioning angle she waited for me to continue. I obliged. "What we see here," I began, "is a dilapidated, bug-infested room in a shamble of a house that should have been torn down years ago. And yet," I continued, "we see clothing neatly folded and placed just so in drawers, a bed made, and luggage placed under it and out of sight. A suit hung up and the shoes, Italian, I might add, nicely polished. Our Mr. Marcos may be all that he is accused of being, but we know he is a man who would be more at home

at the George Cinq than in these squalid surroundings. We are not dealing here with some
lumbering, ham-fisted dockworker," I added,
"but a neat, thorough, and precise adversary.
Someone who must be in control at all times. A
loner, yes, but not to the point that he doesn't
need, if not companionship, then at least the
presence of others around him, as witness his
sojourn tonight down to the local pub. You're
right, Vi," I acknowledged, "in saying he travels light. He fully expected to do his job and be
on his way in no more, I should say, then two
or three days at most."

"That's all very well, I'm sure," announced
my old friend in a slightly belligerent tone. "But
I don't see why it's all so ruddy important to
know his personal habits, like. And another
thing," she continued, turning into the light to
reveal a face wrapped in frown. "What's he
been waiting for, eh? That's what I'd like to
know, right enough."

"In answer to your first question," I stated,
"it's important to know your enemy. It helps to
even the odds. As to your second question, I
can only surmise. There may have been a
change in plans or something gone awry. Either
that or there may be a disagreement over the
money to be paid."

"Well, all I can say," grumbled Vi, "is the
war could be over and done with by the time
we solve anything."

I let the remark pass. And why not? I knew
she was out of sorts and as disappointed as I in
having found nothing concrete to go on. Even
though I was feeling a heightened sense of ex-

citement and yes, even danger, in being in the very room of an international criminal, we were in all respects no farther ahead. "Vi," I suddenly thought to ask, breaking my own train of thought, "that wastebasket by the side of the dresser. You did check it out, didn't you?"

"Had a look at it," she replied. "Filled with nowt but cigarette butts."

"Yes, well, I'll just take a look inside it, shall I?" I asked in an overly pleasant manner, not wishing to upset her any farther by an allegation on my part of an oversight on hers. Placing the wicker basket atop the dresser, I dipped in my hand and, on rummaging around, came up with a small crumpled piece of paper which I carefully unraveled and smoothed out. "It's a message of some sort!" I exclaimed in a twinge of excitement.

"Is it in code?" questioned Vi, hurrying to my side.

"It's cryptic," I answered, "but not in code, thank goodness." Still, I needed time to study it. "Paddy," I called softly over to the window, "any sign of Marcos?"

"Not so much as his shadow," came the cheerful reply.

Dear old Paddy, I'm sure he never fully realized just how dangerous a game we were engaged in. I had the impression he thought of it as no more than a grand and glorious adventure. A tale to be told in the years ahead for the price of a drink. Strange, I thought, to have lived the life he's led and still retain that childlike quality of innocence. I turned my attention

back to Vi. "What do you make of it?" I asked,
passing the note over.

"It's no good you handing it to me," was the
apologetic response. "Needs me reading glasses
for that, I do. You read it," she advised. "I'm
alright for reading things at a distance, like, but
up close—"

"And I," I confessed, "am the exact opposite."

"Well, there you are, you see," she announced with a nudge and a wink. "Between
the two of us—perfect vision."

"Oh, yes, we're perfect, alright," I answered
with a slightly bemused smile. "Two half-blind
old ladies and an alcoholic leprechaun. The perfect team."

"Go, on," she pressed, ignoring my barb,
"read the note."

"It says," I read, " 'Meet R Nov 15 10 pm
Blue something.' "

"Blue something? What's that mean?"

"That's just it. It says, Blue, then something
else. I can't read what. The ink's run from some
sort of water stain on the last part."

"It don't help us much then, does it?" was
the pessimistic response I received. "I mean,"
continued Vi, "who's this here R he's supposed
to meet? We don't know. Where is it they're
supposed to meet? We don't know that either.
I tell you, Emma Hudson," she added with a
weary shake of the head, "if it weren't for bad
luck, we'd have no luck at all."

"I would assume," I stated on a more hopeful
note, "that R is the gentleman who called upon
Marcos when first we set up our surveillance

when you consider that he's been, at least as far as we're aware, his one and only visitor to date."

"Aye, you could be right," she agreed, somewhat reluctantly. "But why would Marcos throw the message away?"

"He wrote it down, committed it to memory, and then disposed of it," I answered. "Very practical, I should say."

"He should have burned it."

"His mistake," I answered with a smile.

"But," added Violet, "we still don't know what all this 'Blue something' business is."

"The Blue Boar," announced our friend from within the shadows.

Being so absorbed in our ongoing dialogue, we had completely forgotten the third member of our trio, and, in truth, his voice caught us off guard as would an unexpected crack of thunder.

"What?" we cried out in startled unison.

"The Blue Boar," he repeated quite casually. "It's the name of a pub not that far from here. Most likely that'd be the one you'd be looking for."

"Paddy," I sang out, in what I must confess was a rare burst of exuberance, "you're a dear!"

"Then again," he added with a self-conscious scratching of the bristled chin, "it just might be the Blue Goose."

"I knew it," moaned Violet.

However, all was not as bleak as my old friend's lamentations would suggest. Having further gleaned from Paddy that both alehouses were in the same area, I put it to both parties that our best course of action would be to separate on the night of the fifteenth—that is to say, two days hence. I, to the Blue Goose, and they, to the Blue Boar. At whatever pub Marcos and friend appear, someone would be there in wait. Questions needed answering. Who was R? Why the meeting? Where would he go after leaving Marcos—home, hotel, or perhaps . . . an embassy? Was he an Afrikaner or an Englishman of dubious loyalty? What mischief was in the making? Oh, yes, many questions, and a scrap of paper found in the bottom of a basket might, in itself, prove to be the first step in unlocking the mystery.

After we had completed a check around the room to see that nothing incriminating had been left behind, I was about to put the scribbled message into my purse when I thought the better of it. Taking pad and pencil in hand, I copied the cryptic note and returned it to the wastebasket. There you are, Mr. Marcos, I thought, quite pleased with myself, everything in its place. Just the way you left it.

SIX

An Incident at the Blue Boar

THE BLUE GOOSE was no worse or, for that matter, no better than a hundred other alehouses stamped, it would seem, out of the same mold. Having taken a table near the door, the better to watch for the arrival of Marcos and friend, I took note that various females would arrive unescorted, then leave at irregular intervals on the arms of male patrons. As proper young ladies would never dream of going out of an evening unless escorted by a gentleman, I observed that the unescorted females in this squalid little setting wasted no little time in acquiring a table partner, for however short the duration. In my own particular case, age, it seems, has its compensations in that society does not look askance at someone of my years either entering or being seated by herself in any such establishment.

While continuing to sip at my drink I turned my attention to the corner off to my left, where a number of patrons were taking an avid interest in a darts tournament currently in progress. I remember William once trying to teach me the rudiments of the game, but I never did quite fully understand, and besides, the attempts I made at throwing darts convinced me it was a game best left to others. Still, I found it fascinating to observe the intense concentration to be seen on the faces of those engaged in the throwing. From what I could gather from their talk, a few of the old salts taking part had at one time or another been asea on Yankee whaling expeditions. Was the board, to them, now a substitute for those mammoth mammals that once they hunted, and the dart, a representation of the harpoon, thrown now with all the skill and deadly accuracy gained from the hurling of those barb-tipped projectiles into the great Leviathans of the deep? Interesting thought. Too interesting, it would seem. So absorbed was I in the watching, I had completely lost all track of time. I glanced upward at the swinging pendulum of a wall clock to my right and was quite taken aback to discover it was now thirteen minutes past ten. I quickly scanned the room, and, while I had never seen his mysterious friend, I knew Marcos by sight well enough. Neither was present. If they were coming, I told myself, they should have arrived by now unless the clock, as in the case of my own watch, was running fast. I leaned over to a group of men hoisting a beer or two at the table next to me. "Do you know the right time?" I inquired of the man closest to me, a ferret-faced individual who, from the glazed look of those beady little eyes, was well into his cups.

"The right time for what, luv?" was the snickering answer I received, accompanied in turn by the loud guffawing of his mates.

Wouldn't you know it. I had to pick the one man who evidently considered himself the comedian of the group. I ignored his remark and began adjusting my coat and gathering up my purse in preparation for leaving.

"Missus?"

I turned to see the youngest of the four, a big, brawny lad yet with a pallor to the skin the color of gray chalk and eyes older than their years, staring up at me.

"Yes?"

"The clock, missus—on the wall," he stated in a voice I could only describe as being reverential in tone (did I represent a mother figure to him?) "it says, fifteen minutes past ten."

"Thank you." I smiled, rising from my chair. "I thought perhaps it was running fast."

"Oh, no," he solemnly informed me. "It's working alright."

"That's more then we can say for you, Archie, m'lad."

It was ferret-face again. Needless to say his quip brought more raucous laughter round the table, save for the young lad named Archie, who sat in embarrassed silence.

I mouthed the words "Thank you, Archie" on passing and made my way to the door. According to Paddy's directions I could make it over to the Blue Boar on foot in less than ten minutes. Boar—Boer? I repeated the word and uttered up a mild oath. Of course! A play on the word "Boer." They *would* meet there, wouldn't they? It would appear our quarry had an ironic sense of humor, and I was the silly goose, blue or not.

Arriving slightly out of breath but none the worse for wear, I elbowed my way in through the milling throng. Evidently, from the size of the crowd, the Blue Boar was the obvious favorite over its aforementioned rival, the Blue Goose, though why this should be was a complete mystery to me. And speaking of mysteries, where, I wondered, were Violet and Paddy? With eyes darting round as I continued my way past sweaty bodies, the smell of stale beer, and layers of blue smoke that hung cloudlike twixt raftered ceiling and floor, leaving me gasping for breath, I was beginning to feel a slight sense of panic setting in. Where *was* she? Was that she? Yes, near the alcove by the bar. Her back was to me, and she appeared to be bending over something or someone. "Vi," I called out on approaching, "what is it? Is anything wrong?"

"Oh, Em," she wailed, turning to me with a most pained expression. "It's that glad I am you're here."

"Why, what's happ—Paddy!" I cried, as she stepped aside to reveal the little man slumped on a chair holding a bloody rag to his forehead. "What on earth! Are you alright?"

" 'Tis nothing but a knock on the noggin." He smiled weakly, trying to put a brave front on it. "Ol' Paddy will be alright, never you mind."

"But you're bleeding!" I exclaimed.

"Right, you two," rang out a voice coming up behind me. "If you're friends of his, see he's out of here quick and proper, like."

I turned to face the voice. "And you are . . . ?" I demanded to know, sizing up a man who, with furrowed brow, droopy eyelids, overly large fleshy earlobes, and wattled neck, reminded me for all the world of an overgrown basset hound. First a ferret, now a hound; this, I told myself, was definitely not my night.

"Billy Burgoyne," he stated defiantly. "I'm the owner of this here establishment. O'Ryan knows me well enough."

"Aye, that I do," spoke Paddy, on attempting to rise. "I know you for what you are, Billy Burgoyne. A man who wouldn't so much as offer a drink to a dying man, such as meself, to save your withered soul."

"You're not dying, O'Ryan."

"But he's been badly hurt," I protested.

"That very well may be," he glowered, "but I run a respectable pub here. I don't want to be muckin' about with no coppers. If they show up and see there's been trouble, they'll start asking questions—well, I mean, it'll upset my customers, won't it."

"Faith, now," replied a mocking Paddy, "we wouldn't be doubtin' for a moment they'd be upset. Especially since the police have files long as an elephant's trunk on half of them what's in here already."

"Funny, ain't you," sneered the publican. "Right, that does it then. I want—"

"One moment, Mr. Burgoyne," I interjected. "We're not taking Mr. O'Ryan anywhere in his present condition. Now, if you've a room . . ."

"There's one right off the alcove round the

corner," Vi was quick to inform me.

" 'Ere," whined Burgoyne, "that's private, that room is."

"Good," I countered. "What we want is privacy. Come along, Violet, Paddy. And you," I stated, addressing those mournful eyes while the hairy hands continued to twist a dirty little hand towel in agitated fashion, "can bring us three brandies and a glass of water."

So saying, in we trooped, with Violet leading the way. No sooner had we settled ourselves round a table than a waiter bearing our drinks entered. "Billy says you've got five minutes," he sullenly informed us before gathering up his tray and exiting.

On his departure, I gave close examination to Paddy's wound. "What in the world happened?" I asked, dipping my handkerchief into the glass of water and gently dabbing away at the dried blood. "Got yourself into a drunken brawl, I'll wager."

"No, it weren't like that at all, Em," announced Vi.

"What, then? Who's responsible for this?"

"Would you be believing me," spoke Paddy with a wince of pain, "if I told you it was himself with no name?"

"Who? I don't—"

"The man Marcos met here tonight," Violet breathlessly informed me. "Our Mr. 'R.' "

"What!" I exclaimed in shocked disbelief. "They've both been here and gone?" They nodded in agreement. "Right," I said, taking a right good swig of my brandy. "Let's have the story from the beginning. Who wants to start? Vi?"

As Vi told it, when entering the Blue Boar with Paddy a few minutes before ten, they found it filled to the rafters, so to speak, with revelers of every size, shape, and description. Although they thought themselves fortunate in finding an unoccupied table at the far end of the room, it had the disadvantage of affording limited visibility of those coming and going by way of the front entrance.

At ten minutes past the hour an old drinking chum spotted Paddy and waved him over to his table. It was on leaving Violet for a word or two with his old shipmate that Paddy spotted Marcos and another man entering the very room in which we sat. His mate was quickly forgotten as Paddy hurried to tell Vi the news. On Violet's suggestion, it was decided in order not to bring undue attention to two people standing outside the hallway with ears pressed against a door, Paddy would make his way over to the room alone in the hope of overhearing what was being said inside, while Violet remained at the table.

"So," said I, with another dab of the hankie to the little man's forehead as my companion ended her part of the tale, "we are now at a point where you are now outside the door, are we?"

"Ah, Mrs. Hudson," he smiled before answering, while I continued to administer to him, "it's a gentle touch you have. A Florence Morningstar, you are."

"Nightingale," I gently corrected him. "Florence Nightingale."

"Ah, well, there you are, you see." (Whatever

that meant.) "Outside the door, you say?" he went on, harking back to my question, rhetorical though it may have been. "I was, that."

"That's an odd cut," I suddenly announced, eyeing the wound as I dabbed away the last of the blood. "It looks like some kind of marking or design. Strange."

"It's not the cut that would be bothering me," he admitted, "so much as the bump on me head when I hit the floor."

"Well, before you go completely crackers, Paddy O'Ryan," exclaimed my impatient friend, "tell us what you heard!"

"Oh, now, Vi," I soothed, "don't be too hard on him. He's had a bad time of it."

"I'll be foin, never you fear," he answered. "All I'd be needin' . . ." He let the words drop, but not the now emptied glass he held.

"Here," I said, offering up with a smile my unfinished drink, "take mine."

I received an impish grin before he quickly downed the remains. "Now, then," he stated, with a wipe of a hand to the mouth, followed by a small belch, "there was meself at the door trying to make out what they were saying inside, just as Mrs. Warner herself had asked."

"And could you?"

"I'd not be lyin', Mrs. Hudson," he confessed, "if I told you only a word or two, here and there. It was Marcos who was bellerin' out for the most part in that queer accent of his. Saying things, he was, like 'I way too long, I way too long,' whatever that might be meaning. I couldn't—"

"Wait a minute," I interrupted. "Could he

have been saying, 'I *wait* too long'?"

"You know, he could at that," acknowledged Paddy, after some thought.

"Right," agreed Vi. "Marcos was that upset because this here other chappie, 'R,' had been putting him off for one reason or another."

"What did our Mr. R sound like?" I asked. "Was he English?"

"He was that, from the sound of him."

"What else could you hear being said?" I questioned, urging him on.

"Faith, this old head can't remember word for word," he answered with an unconscious tugging of his earlobe. "But from what this R fellah was saying, it sounded like he was questioning whether Marcos could—how did he put it?" We waited in silence while he gave yet another tug or two to the ear. "Ah, that'd be it," he said at last. "He was putting it to Marcos whether he could pull it off. His very words, 'pull it off.' "

"Anything else?" I asked hopefully, while continuing to jot down all that was said.

"I remember him saying something about 'days'—'two or three days' or 'a few more days.' But it's like I've been telling you, with all that blatherin' going on in the pub—oh," he added as an afterthought, "it was himself with the accent I heard saying—'You wait, you see, house on Thames go boom.' "

"House on Thames?" Vi and I exchanged puzzled glances.

"I don't know what you would be thinking," he continued, "but to ol' Paddy, this whole thing don't make a crock of sense at all, at all."

"Not yet, at least," I replied. "But this wound you received, how did all that take place?"

"There was meself," he began, "hunched up against the door when suddenly, without so much as a warning, it flew open. The English gent must have been as surprised as meself, for he flings out a curse along with his fist, and I drops to the floor like a bale of cinnamon. The last thing I remember was hearing Marcos asking who I was, and this other gent, or 'R,' as you calls him, saying, 'A drunken sot by the look of him. That'll teach him to go snooping.' Ah," growled Paddy, shaking a liver-spotted fist. "If only I had been ten years younger."

"Then you really never did get a look at this other man—either of you?"

"Just his fist," remarked Paddy.

"But, when you first saw him enter the room?"

"Just a flash of his back," he answered.

"Well, I didn't, how could I, like?" commented Vi, somewhat argumentatively. "When Paddy didn't return I went over to see what had happened to him and found him on the floor. They flashed right by me, they did. But you must have seen them, Em. You came in only a minute or two after they left."

"No," I answered, "I saw no one."

It was a lie. Albeit, a small one. I had seen them though I hadn't realized it at the time. I'd been no more than a few yards away from the Blue Boar when I caught the sound of two men walking at a rather brisk pace toward me. Considering the area, and that we were the only three on the street at that time, plus the fact that a continual light mist had the tendency to turn reality into shadows and shadows into reality, the whole scene had a most nightmarish effect on me. I immediately cast my head downward on their approach. The last thing any woman wants to do under the circumstances I had now found myself in is to establish eye contact, for it strips away that veil of privacy we wrap ourselves in, and we become in that instant no longer faceless blurs but individual personalities to our fellowmen, be they possible assailants or not. It was with that thought in mind I continued on, as I say, with head down and setting myself as brisk a pace as the two now approached even closer. While I never so much as looked up, I could feel their eyes burning into me.

"And you say you never saw them?" repeated Violet.

"No, Mrs. Warner, I did not," I answered. At least, I told myself, not their faces.

Once outside, Paddy assured us he was perfectly capable of making it back to his "digs," as he called them, on his own. As for ourselves, Vi and I agreed the sooner we were away from there the better.

As we stood scanning the empty length of the street for sight or sound of a hansom, a group of ragamuffins approached menacingly from out of the shadows. One little tyke made a grab for Violet's purse, another, for mine. Both angry and shaken, we continued to stand our ground. "Get off, you lot!" cried out Violet. "We'll have the police on you, we will, right enough!" Her protestations were met in turn by jeers and taunts. They now began to circle us as would Red Indians round a wagon train (if Buffalo Bill's Wild West Show is to be believed).

In truth, the situation was definitely getting out of hand when from out of the night the sound of shuffling feet could be heard steadily clomping closer and closer. A silence fell on all as we turned to see, emerging wraithlike out of the mist, a good-sized, broad-shouldered individual with a decided limp, which I suspected was due to a clubfoot, slowly advancing step by dogged step toward us.

In an instant he had lifted the one little ringleader off the ground and was shaking him as vigorously as one would a dog after a bath, before dropping him unceremoniously to the pavement.

"Alright, 'op it now! All of you!" boomed the deep and commanding voice. The little tyke hurriedly picked himself up, and within seconds all had vanished into the back alleys from whence they had come.

We thanked him profusely, and although payment was offered, he would have none of it. For our part, we received a smile accompanied by a tip of his cap before he, too, disappeared into the blackness of the night. As if on cue, a cab arrived on the scene, and, on stepping into it, I directed the cabbie to take us posthaste to 221B Baker Street.

"Well, he were a godsend," breathed Violet with a sigh of relief, as we settled ourselves down for the ride home. "See the way he handled those young jackanapes. I wonder who he was?"

"A guardian angel from the Blue Goose named Archie." I smiled.

SEVEN

Our Hero

⌒AFTER A LIGHT lunch I took myself into the parlor, adjusted a slightly askew antimacassar, and settled down to review my notes of the previous evening. On the glass-topped oval table to the front of me lay my note pad, a pencil, and a sheaf of blank paper. After a rereading I replaced the pad and with pencil in hand wrote down what I imagined had taken place conversationally between Marcos and R, using those words as overheard by Paddy, as reference. When I had finished I had the following account:

Once inside the room Marcos gives vent to his feelings by telling R he is fed up with the delays. "I wait too long! I wait too long!" he repeats angrily and, in like manner, states in no uncertain words his determination to quit himself of England. R tries to calm him down. "Just give it a few more days," he pleads. "Two or three at the most." Marcos is adamant in his

94

refusal to reconsider. Desperate and on the defensive, R retaliates by suggesting that perhaps the "legendary" Marcos is unsure of his own ability. "Having doubts whether you can pull it off, old boy?" he asks. "Is that it?" His question is met with verbal hostility. "You don't worry about Marcos," he tells R, "I know my job! You wait, you see," he adds. "House on Thames go boom." When the meeting is at last terminated, R, playing on his coconspirator's ego, has very cleverly managed to retain the services of Marcos for at least three more days.

As I reread what I had written, it gave me a better sense of what, in all likelihood, had transpired between the two men. I was left with the realization I had been wrong when putting it to Mr. Churchill that the only reason for the delay on their part was either a woman, which I had then dismissed out of hand, or money, which I now dismissed in light of this new information. Indeed, there had been no voices heard raised in anger over payment of any kind throughout the entire meeting. It seemed R was waiting for either something or someone to arrive before a bombing could take place. It had to be either one or the other. Knowing that, at least, I now felt I was on firmer ground. As for a house on the river Thames being blown up, my "firmer ground" gave way to quicksand. Whose house and why? And what purpose, morally or militarily, would it serve the Boers by blowing it up?

As things now stood, I had only three days to track down the house in question. Impossible. My only consolation was that the bombing wouldn't take place today; otherwise, last night's meeting would have concerned itself with time, date, and place. No, it would have to be tomorrow or the day after if it was to take place at all. On that point, I would be less than truthful if I didn't confess I was completely at a loss as how next to proceed.

I might add, it didn't help my thinking process any when I became aware of a mournful wailing filtering down from the floor above. It would seem Mr. Holmes had decided for one reason or another to indulge himself in a tune or two on the violin. Perhaps it wouldn't have been so bad if these miniconcerts of his (that we all were subjected to from time to time) had been either sprightly or melodic; as it was, the residents of 221B Baker were a captive audience for dirges of a most woeful nature. How on earth, I asked myself, does Dr. Watson stand it? As if in answer to my question, the sound of feet could now be heard tramping down the stairs. The good doctor looked in on me in passing and, in lighthearted fashion, shook his head in mock despair before taking himself out the door. After a good fifteen minutes or so, though in truth, it seemed a good deal longer, the music ceased as suddenly as it had begun.

With peace and quiet having once more descended over the Hudson household, I was now able to let my thoughts return to the matter at hand. Mr. Churchill, I decided, should be informed of the intended bomb plot. I would bypass Mr. Henten and cable the information to Mr. Churchill directly, adding that he should disregard the Henten telegram, which the man from the *Morning Post* would have sent by now, stating my previous intention of withdrawing from the case. Having to work through an intermediary was not to my liking, and, in any event, Miles Henten's overall interest in the case struck me as being somewhat less than enthusiastic. Vi and I would go it alone.

Speaking of Violet, what, I wondered, was keeping her? It had been more than an hour since she had left to see whether there was a *Morning Post* to be had at Daisy Whyte's Variety, no more than a block away. No doubt, I smiled to myself, she was busily engaged in a little over-the-counter chin-wag with Daisy herself.

Speak of the devil. In she flounced and, without so much as stopping to remove her coat, made straight down the hall for the kitchen. "Vi," I called out, "in here." A quick retracing of her steps brought her back to the open doors of the parlor, waving a rolled-up newspaper about in a most agitated fashion. "Oh, Em," she cried in a manner twixt excitement and distress, "have you heard the news?"

"What news?"

" 'Bout Mr. Churchill," she announced, sinking down in the chesterfield beside me. "Oh, it's just awful, it is."

My heart sank. Could it be that this fine young man with a most promising future ahead of him was now a casualty of a war that had already claimed the lives of too many other fine young men? How senseless it all seemed. But I am a woman and know nothing of the glory

men find in disposing of one another on the
field of honor. I mentally pictured his lifeless
body staring upward with unseeing eyes into
the heart of an African sun. "He's dead," I said,
slowly and evenly. "Is that what you're trying
to tell me?"

"Dead? No, nothing like that," she declared.
"He's been captured, he has."

"Captured?" My heart soared. "Thank God,
for that, at least."

"Everybody down at Daisy's were talkin'
about it. Here," she added, quickly spreading
the paper out before me, "read about it yourself."

Taking paper in hand, I read where Mr.
Churchill had been aboard a train carrying ar-
mored vehicles and troops that subsequently
had the misfortune of being derailed by a Boer
ambush. Under a hail of bullets our Mr. Churchill had advanced to the engine to direct op-
erations for the clearing of the track. That
having been accomplished, the engine, although unable to hook up to the derailed carriages, escaped under her own steam with the
wounded aboard, while Mr. Churchill and the
remaining outnumbered troops, after a brief
skirmish, were quickly rounded up and taken
prisoner.

I smiled in silent admiration. A most remark-
able young man. "If Mr. Churchill were seeking
to make a name for himself," I remarked, "he's
certainly done that. He's turned out to be quite
the hero."

"Aye," agreed Vi. "It's in all the papers. I was

lucky, I was, to get a *Post*. It's the last one Daisy had left."

"Is there any news as to what happened to him since being taken prisoner?"

"Farther down," she answered, pointing to the paper, "it says something about him being sent to someplace called Pretoria for the duration of the war."

So much, I thought, for the sending of a cable. I was about to cast the paper aside when an item at the bottom caught my eye. "What's this?" I said aloud.

"What?"

"It says a man's body has been found washed up on the banks of the Thames near Waterloo Bridge."

"A suicide then, was it?"

"Not necessarily," I answered. " 'Due to the fact," I read on, "that no identification was to be found on the body and with an injury to the head inconsistent with a drowning, the police are reviewing the death as a possible murder.' Then it goes on," I continued, "to describe the victim as being in his early twenties, of medium height with brown hair and, aside from a mole on the left side of the cheek, no other identifying marks were to be found on the body."

" 'Ere, now," spoke Vi, viewing me with some suspicion, "I hope you're not thinking of getting us involved. I mean, we've enough to do already, we have, what with—"

"No, no," I was quick to reassure her, "my point is that a young man, possibly the victim of a murder, rates no more than a two-inch column while Mr. Churchill's exploits—well, you see what I mean."

"Ah, well, it's the same old story, ain't it? Give the people what they want. Though we all needs a hero, Em," she added, "especially in these times."

"I suppose you're right," I reluctantly agreed with a sigh.

"Well, I'd best be putting my coat away," announced my companion on rising. "Then I'll make us both a nice cup of tea, if you like."

"Yes," I smiled, "I'd like that."

As we continued to discuss the case over tea and biscuits it occurred to me that something was out of kilter with the events that had taken place the previous night. I put it to Vi that I found it odd that Marcos would have shown up at all at the Blue Boar.

"Why's that?"

"When last I spoke to Mr. Henten," I explained, "it was agreed he would inform Scotland Yard of the man's presence and where he was lodged. Yet," I went on, "we find Marcos showing up, nice as you please, with his coconspirator at one of the local pubs."

"So, you're saying this here Henten never so much as bothered to call the Yard, right?"

"That's the way it looks. But why? If they had taken him into custody for extradition proceedings," I continued, "we wouldn't have to concern ourselves with trying to solve where a bombing is to take place."

"Well, he's a newspaperman, ain't he?" she answered, as if that explained everything. "I mean," she went on, noting my questioning look, "he's hoping to catch this here Marcos in the act so's he can be the big flamin' hero, same as our Mr. Churchill. That's what I think."

"But a bombing." I shook my head in disbelief. "He could be putting people's lives at risk. In any event," I stated quite firmly, "there is only one thing to do."

"Aye, and what's that?"

Before an answer could be given Dr. Watson returned and, along with a nod in our direction, emitted a small sigh of relief on noting that the strains of a violin were no longer to be heard within the house.

"Now, what was that you were saying?" asked Vi, turning back to me as the doctor made his way up the stairway to his chambers.

"As soon as I finish my tea," I announced, "I'm off to Scotland Yard to inform Inspector Lestrade himself where he can pick up Marcos. And that," I stated, "should be the end of it."

"You mean the case is closed?"

"Just as soon as he's in custody," I answered. "I've no doubt the inspector will have him behind bars in jig time."

Having known the man from the Yard from his frequent visits to Mr. Holmes over the years, I had found him to be a very genial gentleman with always an inquiring word or two as to the state of my well-being. And although his powers of deduction, as outlined by Dr. Watson in his writings of those cases both he and Mr. Holmes were involved in, were no match for the master criminologist's, I had always found him to be, in his own plodding way, thorough, precise, and ever the dedicated professional.

On rising from the chesterfield, I noticed through the curtained window a familiar figure making his way toward the house from across the street. "I thought our Mr. O'Ryan was over on Tench Street keeping watch," I remarked.

"Aye, that's right. Far as I know, at least."

"Then it must be his double," I smiled, advancing toward the vestibule. "Paddy, come in, come in," I welcomed him on opening the door. "And how's that head of yours today?"

"And haven't I had hangovers that were worse," he announced, smiling that gap-toothed smile of his. "But it's kind of you it is to ask, Mrs. Hudson," he added, stepping just inside and removing his cap.

"Well, don't just stand there," I gently admonished him. "Mrs. Warner and I were just having tea, perhaps . . . ?"

"Tea?" His face sagged. "Ah, thank you, no, I never touch the stuff this early in the day. The thing of it is," he went on to explain, "I've just dropped by to let you and Mrs. Warner know that that Marcos fellow has, in a manner of speaking, pulled up anchor and cast off."

"You mean—"

"Aye, checked clean out of his lodgings, he has. Ol' Paddy's been doing a little snooping on his own, you might say," he very confidentially informed me. "Seems he up and left sometime yesterday morning."

"Then he's gone back to wherever he came from," spoke Violet, on joining us at the door. "And the better we are for it."

"Gone back?" I remarked, voicing my

thoughts aloud. "I don't think so. If he were leaving the country, why bother to show up for a meeting at the Blue Boar the same day he checked out?"

"Then . . ."

"Perhaps something scared him off, or perhaps," I mused, "he's being doubly cautious."

"Well, I'll be leaving it up to you two ladies to be figuring it out," spoke Paddy, clamping cap to head.

"You're on your way? But how will we get in touch with you? With Marcos gone, there's no point in going back to our lookout over on Tench."

"Ah, well, that's just it, you see. I've been thinking of bunking down there, seeing as how you and Mrs. Warner have made it snug and cozylike."

"Snug and cozy!" exclaimed Vi. "With nowt but two chairs and a crate for a table? It don't take much to please the likes of you, Paddy O'Ryan."

"At least," I added knowingly, "it's rent-free until someone finds you out."

"That's it, you see." He winked. "But never you be worrying yourselves. Ol' Paddy will be around whenever you needs him."

"Wait," I said, and returning with purse in hand placed two pound notes into the pocket of his jacket. "You've done noble duty, Mr. O'Ryan and," I went on to assure him, "there'll be something for that other pocket as well when this case is finally solved."

The red-veined cheeks deepened into vermilion as the grizzled face registered surprise and flustered excitement. "And may all the saints in heaven smile down on the both of you for being the grand ladies that you are," he managed to sputter out.

Having bestowed his blessings upon us, and with nothing more to be said, he went happily on his way.

"What do we do now?" I asked of Violet on reentering the parlor.

"Well, for one thing," she answered, "we've got some peas out in the kitchen that need shelling."

What was I to do with that woman? "Oh, Vi," I moaned, "I mean, what do we do now, about the case? There's no point," I explained, "in calling on the inspector when we no longer know the whereabouts of Marcos; just as there's no point in sending Mr. Churchill a cable he'll never receive."

"Funny, ain't it?"

"Funny? Funny?" I repeated. "I see nothing funny about it at all."

"I mean," she went on, "there's our Mr. Churchill locked up in some jail, he is, over there in darkest Africa, and there's this here Marcos running about London, free as a bird."

"It's odd, it's ironic," I snapped, "but it's not funny."

" 'Ere," she drew back, "there's no need to be gettin' testy, like. I only meant—"

"Oh, I'm sorry, Vi," I apologized. "But it's all been so frustrating. It seems this whole case so far has been one of two steps forward and three steps back." I plunked myself down and took a sip from the remains of my tea. Stone cold. I made a face.

"What, summat wrong with the tea, then?"

"On top of everything else," I remarked, very straight-faced, "the tea's cold. Funny, ain't it?"

At that last remark, Vi gave me the oddest look then, on detecting a glimmer of a smile that I could no longer hold back, we both burst out laughing like two silly schoolgirls.

Entering the kitchen, Violet made mention that Daisy Whyte had a favor to ask of me.

"A favor?"

"Aye. She wants to know, what with you and her being the same size and all, if she could borrow your coat for tonight."

"Tonight? Yes, I don't see why not."

"Oh, she'll be ever so pleased, she will," smiled my old friend with a sigh of relief. "I told her you would."

"What's the occasion?"

"It's a special night for her, you might say."

"A special night?" I smiled. "It wouldn't have anything to do with a certain Mr. Walgreen, the chemist, now would it?"

" 'Ere, how'd you know that?"

"My dear, Mrs. Warner," I knowingly replied, "it's been common gossip throughout the neighborhood that our Mr. Walgreen has been casting lovesick eyes in Daisy's direction ever since her husband passed away over a year ago. And now he's finally screwed up his courage to ask her out, has he? Imagine," I exclaimed, while in the process of dumping handfuls of podded peas on the counter, "Daisy, with a beau! Why, she must be our age, at least."

"Aye, she's that alright," agreed Violet.
"Which only goes to prove, Emma Hudson,
there's hope for us yet."

Adhering to the old adage "too many cooks
spoil a broth" we had agreed that Vi and I
would take turns each night preparing supper.
As this was my night, Violet made herself comfortable at the kitchen table while I scurried
about in preparation for the evening meal. But
my thoughts, I'm afraid, were not on the sim-
mering pot roast. The thing of it was, I couldn't
get Miles Henten out of my mind. He seemed
to weave in and out of our investigation like
some vaporous fog. How I would have liked to
have had a good old-fashioned, sit-down, face-
to-face, question-and-answer session with him.
And, oh, there were so many questions. Why
had he not informed Scotland Yard of Marcos?
Did he know the man had checked out of his
flat? If yes, did he know where his new lodgings were located? Had he heard anything
about a house on the Thames being the target
for a bombing? Had he found out who it was
that Marcos was working for? And, on a personal note, did he have access to any inside information regarding Mr. Churchill's well-being,
other than what had been written in the papers?
And so on, and so on.

All this was assuming, of course, he had, as
Violet had suggested, decided to carry on with
the case. Or he might very well have made up
his mind to chuck it all, as he gave every indication of doing when last we met.

Like it or not, Miles Henten was our last
hope. And, I told myself, if I wanted to confront

him to find out what, if anything, he knew, I'd never do it from the kitchen of 221B Baker Street. When I put these thoughts forward to Vi, it was agreed I should take myself down to the offices of the *Post* for a meeting with our vaporous Mr. Henten.

"Never you worry 'bout supper, luv," announced Vi. "I'll see to it. But if you want to make it over there 'fore they close up shop for the night, you best be leaving now."

And I did.

EIGHT

A Terrible Tragedy

꩜ONCE INSIDE THE entrance of the *Morning Post* I made my way across a green-tiled lobby floor to a waist-high oak wood counter complete with swinging gate. Behind the counter I could see rows of desks at which sat studious-looking men busily engaged in clanging away in a most furious fashion at big, black metal typewriters. I observed with a quick glance around the office that Mr. Henten was nowhere to be seen. Noting a few desks were devoid of human occupancy, I thought, with some distress, that perhaps he had been among those who had left early for the day. Not knowing quite what to do next, I turned my attention to an old gentleman standing behind the counter whose bald head, save for a few care-fully plastered-down strands of hair atop his dome, was bent over a sheaf of papers, seem-ingly oblivious to all around him. I waited for a moment or two as he went about the reading and rearranging of the material before making my presence known with a slight clearing of the throat and an added, "Excuse me."

A sallow, sunken-cheeked countenance encompassing gray, watery eyes stared up at me over small circular eyeglasses that came to rest halfway down a nose that seemed to go on forever.

"Can I help you, madam?" asked the cadaverous face.

"Yes," I said. "I was hoping to see Mr. Henten, Mr. Miles Henten."

"You are not alone in that hope, madam," he answered a trifle sardonically.

His answer confused me. Did I have another mystery on my hands? "I don't understand," I said.

"Had you made a prior appointment?" he asked, ignoring my query.

"Ah, no, I'm a friend of the family," I lied, hoping I might elicit more information if I pretended my business was of a more personal nature.

"I didn't know young Henten had a family," he responded in what I took to be a slightly suspicious tone of voice.

"Yes, well, I'm a relative, actually," I blurted out. "An aunt—his only living relative," I added, surprising myself as I continued to build upon my story. "I'm in London only for a few days, and I was hoping to see him before I left."

"I see." The bald pate began to nod knowingly. "Under those circumstances I suppose it's only right you should know he's not been seen in the office for the last few days."

"Not seen? Is he sick?"

"If he is, he should have sent word to that effect," he stated most officiously, before adding in a whispered aside, "Mind you, it doesn't mean tuppence to me, Mrs. . . . ?"

"Hudson."

"Hudson, but from what I hear, if he hasn't put in an appearance by tomorrow, he'll be for it, if you get my drift."

"Could it be," I suggested, "he's on some sort of secret assignment?"

"Secret assignment?" he repeated with a light chuckle in a face I venture never smiled easily or often. "Why, bless me, madam, our Mr. Henten writes the obituaries. Secret assignment, indeed," he tut-tutted.

I found myself mentally staggered by this revelation. "Excuse me, Mr. . . . ?"

"Farnsworth, Mrs. Hudson. Chief accountant for the *Morning Post*."

"Excuse me, Mr. Farnsworth, but are we talking about the same Miles Henten? He is a friend of Mr. Churchill, is he not?"

"Yes, I would say so," he acknowledged. "The two seemed to hit it off right enough as business acquaintances. Though I would not expect to see the two of them dining together at the Savoy," he added, "if you get my drift."

"Yes, quite. But, still . . ."

"Yes?"

There was something queer going on, but what? "Would you have his home address?" I asked, in the hope of—in the hope of anything, I suppose.

"Oh, we're not allowed to give out that sort of information," he stated, as a forefinger pushed the eyeglasses up to the bridge of the nose. "You, yourself, don't have it?" he asked, more out of curiosity than suspicion, I think.

"I only knew he worked at the *Morning Post*," I replied, which in itself was true.

He left it at that and announced that when Mr. Henten did arrive, he would inform that gentleman I had been inquiring about him.

"And Mr. Churchill," I thought to ask, "the *Post* has heard nothing more of him?"

"No, and I don't suppose we shall. At least," he went on, gathering up his papers, "not until this mess in South Africa is cleared up. Nasty business, that. Now, if you'll excuse me, I should be getting back to my office and away from all this continual clattering, if you get my drift."

"A roomful of typewriters can be quite disconcerting," I agreed. "Still, we can't stop progress."

"And more's the pity for that!" he snorted. "Though I was heartened to hear recently that some member of Parliament suggested the patent office be closed down as he believes there is nothing more to be invented. I pray that he's right. Motorcars, telephones, typewriters," he continued on in the same crusty manner, "nothing more than fads of the day. A word of warning, madam," he cautioned me, "don't throw away your quill pen just yet, if you get . . ."

"Yes, Mr. Farnsworth." I smiled. "I get your drift."

"I wonder what he's up to? I mean his not showing up for work, and all," Violet said after we had cleared away the supper dishes and made ourselves comfortable in the parlor.

"I'm afraid we've come to a dead end with Mr. Miles Henten," I acknowledged with a sigh. "This whole affair has been most frustrating."

"Aye, well, at least we haven't heard of any bomb going off. If there had been, there'd be newsboys on every corner hawking extra editions quicker than you could say Bob's your uncle."

"True. But I fear the fuse is getting shorter. And if I'm right, we've but a day left before some poor creature and his house is blown to smithereens. We seem," I added, on an equally disparaging note, "to have had more than our fair share of bad luck on this one."

"I've been thinking about that, I have," replied Vi, in a most curious tone.

"About . . . ?"

"Now, I'm not mentioning any names, mind you," she assured me, "but there's a certain little Irishman I'm beginning to have my doubts about."

"What!" I blurted out. "Paddy? Oh, Vi, you can't be serious."

"I'm serious, right enough," she announced defensively. "Well, I mean, when you think back to Shandling's and him turning up out of the blue like that, so to speak. And then," she went on, becoming more animated in her gestures, "finding that room opposite Marcos's lodgings like he did and then picking that lock, nice as you please, so's we'd be able to find the message. Probably wrote it, too," she added, "if it comes to that."

She left me completely bewildered. "But Vi," I reasoned, "in the first place, the man's illiterate. He couldn't even read the note, let alone write it. And in the second place," I continued, "his actions have proved more than helpful on more than one occasion."

"Well, it all seems a little too convenient, if you ask me," she sniffed. "I think he's in cahoots with 'em, is what I think."

"I see. And that's why they gave him a bloody head, is it?" I responded with a touch of sarcasm.

"That," she replied very knowingly, "was so we wouldn't get suspicious of him, like. Oh, yes," she assured me, "figured it all out, I have."

What could I say? Violet Warner could be as stubborn as the proverbial mule, and once she set her mind to something there wasn't much twixt heaven and earth that could change it. She had her suspicions, and that was that. "Well," I diplomatically suggested, "if you feel that way, we best keep a closer eye on him." While she appeared to be somewhat mollified by my overture, I felt a change of subject would not be amiss. "What would you say to having a telephone installed in the house?" I asked.

"A telephone!" was the startled response. "Why, Emma Hudson, how could you ever think of such a thing?"

Evidently it was the wrong subject.

"A telephone, indeed," she harrumphed while straightening out the folds in her dress in an exaggerated and agitated fashion. "They're the devil's own instrument, they are. All that electricity running through a wire and ending up in your ear, why, it's not natural, like."

"But, Vi, you don't under—"

"You can say what you want," she cut in, "but it's not for me, luv, thank you, very much."

"You don't happen to know a Mr. Farnsworth, do you?" I asked with a smile, thinking back to that equally conservative gentleman.

"Who?"

The question, interrupted by a knocking at the door, was never answered.

"That'll be Daisy, like as not, come to borrow your coat," sang out Violet, relieved as I that a third party had ended any further discussion of telephones.

Daisy Whyte was a dear old soul though I use that term not in any way condescendingly, for the woman would be no more than a year or two older than I and, I must admit, endowed with, to coin a phrase, a most heavenly peaches and cream complexion. True, like the rest of us, the "peach" may have become somewhat wrinkled over the years, but it did have the most enviable glow to it. Still, with eyes of pale green set a little too close to the nose and the mouth a little too large for the face, it is doubtful if she was ever considered pretty even as a young woman. Yet, with time having softened the features and being possessed of a warm, outgoing personality coupled with a smile that melted years from her face, it was easy to see why a certain Wallace Walgreen had set his cap for her.

"Daisy, come in, come in," I beckoned with a smile as she entered the parlor just to the back of Vi. "And how have you been keeping yourself of late?" I asked, as she seated herself in the chair opposite.

"Oh, I can't complain, Mrs. Hudson. 'Course," she added with a laugh, "I don't suppose it would help much if I did, would it?"

I noted that while she had no compunction in addressing Violet by her Christian name, my repeated attempts over the years to have her call me Emma had proved futile. I believe my being mentioned on more than one occasion in Dr. Watson's stories on Mr. Holmes elevated me, at least in Daisy's mind and in some respect the minds of our neighbors, a rung or two up their social ladder. Though far be it for me to play the Grand Dame of Baker Street.

"Oh, isn't it terrible about poor Mr. Churchill," she twittered. "I was ever so shocked to read he'd been captured. Vi, here, says that he'd been to this very house 'fore he went off to Africa to do his bit for the war."

I shot my companion an icy stare. Had she been telling the entire street of our latest venture? Were we now to add to the team of Hudson and Warner, the butcher, the baker, and candlestick maker?

"I only mentioned," spoke Vi, who evidently had read my mind, "that he dropped by, like."

I breathed a sigh of relief. "Yes, on some business or other with Mr. Holmes, as I recall," I added in an offhanded manner.

"Still, all in all," she continued, "Mr. Churchill. I mean, meet all kinds of interesting people, you do. Many's the time I've stood behind the counter looking out the window and seen carriages with their fancy crests pull up outside your door. Mind you," she quickly added, "it's not that I'm spying, so to speak, but you can't help noticing something special like that, can you?"

"Speaking of something special," I teased, "you've been having someone special dropping by the shop on more than one occasion and for more than just a pouch of tobacco, from what I hear."

"Who? Oh," she answered as two little blotches of red appeared on those creamy cheeks, "you mean, Mr. Walgreen. Well, yes," she fidgeted, "I did say I'd go out with him. Not," she added, perhaps a little too quickly, "that it means anything, of course."

"Of course not," we solemnly responded.

"But," she went on, "since he did mention taking me to some posh restaurant tonight, I thought perhaps, that is, if I could . . ."

"Borrow my coat? Yes, of course," I responded. "Vi mentioned it earlier."

"Oh, I'm ever so grateful, Mrs. Hudson," she answered with a smile that quickly faded as the eyes took on a lost, haunted look for just the briefest of seconds.

There was something wrong. I could sense it from the moment she walked in. The laugh was a little too forced, and the gestures, while I wouldn't describe them as frenetic, were a tad fidgety. Overall, she presented herself to me as being preoccupied with troubled thoughts that lay elsewhere. If she had not been an old friend, I would not have mentioned it. As she was . . .

"Is there anything wrong?" I asked.

"Wrong?" was the startled reply. "Why, no, Mrs. Hudson."

" 'Ere, now, Daisy, you should know by now if Emma Hudson believes there's summat wrong, summat's wrong," stated Vi, before asking, "Had a bit of a to-do with your Mr. Walgreen, then, did you?"

"No, nothing like that, Violet," she remonstrated. "But you're right, Mrs. Hudson," she confessed, "there has been something troubling me."

I said nothing. If she wanted to unburden herself farther, the choice was hers.

"The thing of it is . . ." She hesitated for a moment, looking first to me and then Vi before asking, "Do you believe in dreams?"

I was completely taken aback. Of all the questions in the world, I hadn't expected that one. "Dreams?" I repeated. "Well, I don't know, really. I suppose it depends on the dreamer. If a dream comes true, one tends to believe. If it doesn't, one tends to think of it as being nothing more than fragmented memories. A jigsaw puzzle, if you will, with the pieces in all the wrong places. Nothing more, nothing less."

"You can say what you want about dreams, Em," announced Vi, "but I had one I'll never forget. It were a nightmare, really. No more than a child I was," she went on, with no urging I assure you from either Daisy or myself. "I'd been asleep I don't know for how long when I dreamed I saw my Uncle Wilbur, who was living in Leeds at the time, having moved there after divorcing my Aunt Jane and oh, wasn't that a scandal at the time—though I always liked him, Wilbur being my favorite uncle and all. Anyway, like I say, there were Uncle Wilbur, or Uncle Willy as I called him as a child, standing by the window, leastways in my dream he was, and looking all pale and ghostly, like. But he were smiling, you see, as if to tell me he was feeling right as rain and not to worry. Then, nice as you please, he ups and floats out the window. Aye," she assured us, "it's summat I'll not forget. Fair scared me half to death, it did—little thing that I was."

"And you learned the following day your uncle had suddenly passed away in the night, did you?" I asked, having been caught up in her telling of the tale.

"Well, no, not exactly, like," she hedged. "Actually he died three years later—struck down by a runaway horse. Still, all in all . . ."

"Oh, Vi," was my exasperated comment, with anything else I could have thought to add being cut short by Daisy remarking, "Leastways, I can understand her being frightened. I know that feeling, right enough."

"Then yours too," I asked, "is more of a nightmare than a dream, is it?"

"And a horrible one at that, Mrs. Hudson."

"Is this a recurring nightmare you have, or . . . ?"

"It's one I've had to live through every night for the last five nights. And if it doesn't end soon," she added with trembling lip, "I'm afraid to think what I shall do."

As Vi poured her a cup of tea I made the suggestion that perhaps if she told us about it, it might help in easing her mind, adding that any frightening event, whether mental or physical, takes on a less sinister aspect when it is a shared experience. She nodded in agreement, reset cup to saucer, and, after a moment or two to regain her composure, related the following:

"It's always the same. I find I'm walking down a street. There's not a soul to be seen. What street it is, I don't know. It might even be Baker. I'm not sure what time it is, only that it's night, very cold and foggy, and I want to go home. I know if only I can make it back to my house, I'll be safe. But, safe from what? And then I hear them. Footsteps. They're in back of me. I want to turn around and look, but I'm too frightened. I pull my coat collar up around me and begin to walk faster. As I do, I hear the footsteps quicken their pace. Then, without warning, I'm grabbed from behind. My head's pulled back, and I feel a terrible pain in my throat. My tongue feels thick. I want to cry out, but I can't. Then everything goes black." She gave a little shiver, reached for her cup, drained its contents, and sat back. "That's all, I'm afraid," she said, trying to conjure up a wisp of a smile. "After that, I wake up. Silly, isn't it?"

"Silly? I should say not!" I exclaimed.

"And there was me rattlin' on 'bout Uncle Wilbur and all," added Vi. "And all the while you've been keeping inside summat like that."

"But what does it all mean?" she asked, with eyes that pleaded for an answer.

"I think, perhaps," I ventured, "that you've been under a great deal of stress lately. When was it that Mr. Walgreen first asked you out?"

"Why," she replied, "it was no more than a week ago. Why?"

"Well, there you are, you see." I smiled.

"What's this you're saying!" was the incredulous response from Vi. "That Daisy's Mr. Walgreen is out to do her in?"

"Not at all," I hastened to assure my companion. "Keep in mind that this is her first outing with a man, other than her late husband, since the days before her marriage. Couple that with her anxiety about what she'll wear, do, and say. Add to that," I went blithely on, "the daily chore of trying to make a go of the shop on her own and, well, there you are. All the fears and frustrations bottled up inside with no place to go."

"Do you really believe that's all that it is?" asked Daisy.

"Why, of course," I replied in a comforting tone. "Get out and enjoy yourself more, Daisy Whyte. It'll do you the world of good."

Did I really believe all that I had told her? Perhaps not. But in any event, it seemed to satisfy her, and I suppose that's all that really mattered. "Now, m'girl," I said, escorting her to the hall closet, "let's get that coat for you, shall we? And I've just the hat to go with it."

Happily, the coat, except for being a tad too tight at the shoulders, fitted her perfectly, as did the hat. After being showered with a profusion of "thank-you's" we saw her to the door, where she hesitated long enough to inquire, "Is he in?"

"Who?" we asked.

"Mr. Holmes," she replied, peeking past Violet toward the staircase.

"Why, no," I answered. "He went out sometime earlier. Why do you ask?"

"Oh, I would so have liked to see him," she gushed. "What with him being so well-known, and all."

"Well, we don't keep him on display like he were in some kind of wax museum," responded Vi with a good-natured chuckle.

"Oh, Violet," she burst forth with what I noted was the first really genuine laugh I'd heard from her all evening, "you are a caution, you are. You almost make me afraid to ask if Dr. Watson . . . ?"

"Yes, the doctor is in," I was quick to inform her, "but he doesn't like to be disturbed on an evening."

"Oh. Well, I do have this pain—"

"By appointment only, luv," was Vi's wry comment.

And so it was with yet another goodbye and a wish that she enjoy her evening with Mr. Walgreen, that we watched Daisy, decked out in my Inverness coat and cloche hat, with one last wave goodbye, set off down the street.

As we reentered the parlor I put it to Vi that our best course of action at this juncture would be to gather our notes together with whatever bits of information we had accumulated during the course of our investigation and sit down

and sort out what we knew and didn't know;
in other words, thrash it out to see just where
we stood since, as I believed, we had precious
little time left. No sooner had we settled ourselves than we caught the sound of a police-
man's whistle breaking the stillness of the
night. "I wonder what that's all about?" I
asked, turning my attention toward the window. "It doesn't sound that far off."

"Probably some gent what's got his wallet
nicked, like as not."

"I don't think so. It sounds more serious than
that," I added above the whistle's continual
sharp, staccato blasts. "Listen."

Outside, the cry of voices, though barely audible inside the confines of our room, could be
heard calling out a singular word that sent a
shiver through the two of us.

"Did you hear that?" asked Vi, as we stood
at the parted curtains peering out into the dimly
gaslit street. "Did they say—"

" 'Murder'? Yes. Look, you can make out
people running in the direction of the whistle
blast. C'mon, m'girl," I said, quickly grabbing
an old cloth coat of mine from the hall closet,
"we best have a look-see." Just before heading
out I mentioned that perhaps it might be best if
one of us inform Dr. Watson, as his presence
might be required. Violet volunteered, and, as
she turned back toward the staircase, I ventured
out onto the street toward an already milling
throng. As I edged my way through I saw our
neighborhood guardian, Constable Hurley,
whom I had always found to be both a pleasant and dedicated young chap, doing his best

to control a crowd of onlookers who had seemingly materialized as if out of nowhere. "Constable Hurley," I called out, "what's happened?"

"Oh, it's you, Mrs. Hudson," he replied, and with a harried look added, "Is Mr. Holmes with you?"

I took it his question was prompted by the situation at hand. Being no more than a recent recruit himself, and, with no senior officer having arrived as yet on the scene, it was understandable he should desire the presence of Mr. Holmes.

"No," I answered on approaching, "but Dr. Watson will be along shortly should you have need of him." It was at that point that I had my first glimpse of the victim—a woman—whose crumpled body lay on the dampened street with the back of her head toward me. Was she alive or dead? It was a question I asked myself as I stood transfixed in a combination of mute horror and fascination as a thin ribbon of red seeping out from under the back of her head continued to undulate its way over cobbled stones before coming to rest in a small pool at the base of my feet. It was a sight I could have endured more easily had I not spotted the hat that lay no more than a foot away from her head. A cloche hat. My hat. "Dear, God, in heaven!" I gasped. "It's not Daisy, is it? Daisy Whyte?" I had no need for an answer, for I had now recognized my Inverness coat which she had borrowed and been the proud possessor of but a short time before.

"Yes, Mrs. Hudson," spoke the constable,

"I'm sorry to say it is. Always had a kind word and a sweet or two for me, Mrs. Whyte did, whenever I'd pop into her shop. And now this," he added. "And for what, I ask you? A few bob?"

"Then the motive was robbery?"

"Well, what else could it be?"

"I believe that's her handbag," I said, directing my gaze to the object that lay to the left of her foot. "Was anything taken?"

"What little money she had is still there," he answered, then noting an arched eyebrow from yours truly—"Oh, I see what you mean," was the flustered response. "Yes, well, like as not the culprit panicked, you might say, and ran off soon as the deed was done."

I nodded but said nothing, except, "Is she . . . ?" I couldn't bring myself to say the word, fearing in a childlike way that if I did, it would be so.

"Dead? No, she's alive, Mrs. Hudson, but just barely."

"Thank God for that at least," I answered with a heartfelt sigh of relief. "Here," I said, taking off my coat and bundling it up, "I'll just slip this under her head." As I bent down I saw, with a heavy heart, that that once creamy complexion was now a pasty white. My ministrations also gave me the opportunity to observe for the first time the nature of the wound. As I did, I went completely numb, and for a moment felt as if I were about to faint. Her throat had been slashed! In that instant her words came tumbling back over me. "I'm walking down a street . . . my head's pulled back . . . there's a terrible pain in my throat." It was no nightmare she'd experienced, but a premonition. A premonition of her own death. "Daisy, it's Mrs. Hudson," I cried aloud into that immobile face. "Don't give up! Dr. Watson is on his way." In response I received the slightest flicker of an eyelid, and nothing more.

"Here's the doctor now, Mrs. Hudson," spoke the constable as he assisted me to my feet. "Alright, you lot!" he barked, turning once more to the crowd as they sought to edge in closer. "Make way for the doctor."

How ironic, I thought, while Daisy and the doctor would at last meet, only one would be aware of the encounter. On his approach I expressed my thanks for coming so quickly and, after Constable Hurley had filled him in as to what had taken place, as well as to the extent of her injuries, the good doctor eased himself down on one knee beside the poor woman, unlatched his medical bag, and began an intensive examination of the wound. Off in the distance a clanging of bells accompanied by the sound of galloping hooves announced the imminent arrival of an ambulance.

Violet, standing on the periphery of the crowd, her face contorted in anguish as a handkerchief repeatedly dabbed watery eyes, would come no closer. I took her by the arm, and, together, in silence, we made our way back home.

"I wish we had something a little stronger," I announced, pouring the remains of my cooking sherry into two glasses.

"A wink's as good as a nod," answered Vi, trying to summon up a smile.

We sipped in solitude. Had I, I thought, been too glib when first told of Daisy's nightmare? Might it not have happened if I had taken her more seriously? Was there something I could have done that I hadn't? If yes, what? I tried to comfort myself that as some believe our destiny is preordained at birth, then neither I nor anyone else could have done anything to save her. Or is that nothing more than merely a rationalization for evading responsibility to one's fellow human beings? Am I not my brother's (sister's) keeper?

These thoughts and more were broken off by the sound of a key being turned in the front door lock signaling the return of Dr. Watson. Presenting himself within the parlor, along with my coat that had pillowed that poor woman's head, he gently broke the news that Daisy Whyte had expired only minutes after we had taken our leave. Extending condolences, he solemnly bade us good night before once more retiring to his room.

"It's just not right, summat like that happening," uttered my companion in an emotionally drained voice. "Murdered for a bit of loose change, the constable said. What's the world coming to, I wonder," she added, staring deep into the now empty cup as if it were some kind of crystal ball that could magically supply all the answers.

Poor Violet. What had been so blatantly clear to me had completely escaped her. Daisy Whyte, a woman of my height and build, wearing my coat and hat, is done away with in cold blood minutes after emerging from 221B Baker Street. It doesn't take a Sherlock Holmes or, if I may be so bold, an Emma Hudson, to see who the intended victim was to have been.

Me.

NINE

The House on the Thames

ⅎTHE FOLLOWING DAY the sun, having taken off for parts unknown, left in its stead a perfectly frightful dead gray sky. I gazed in sympathy out the kitchen window at the spruce I had planted in the backyard a little over three years ago swaying now in solitary helplessness to a wind whistling mournful tunes through its naked branches, in turn, creating a bleak and somber mood outside, matched only in kind by the two occupants inside.

Since breakfast, the death of Daisy Whyte had been given only passing reference by Violet as well as myself. It was as if we had both mentally agreed that to relive it again would be too soon and too emotional an experience. There'd be time enough for tears later. However, as we settled ourselves down at the kitchen table, Vi had one final comment to make in regard to that most unhappy event of the previous evening.

"About last night," she began a trifle hesitantly, which in itself was so unlike her that she immediately piqued my interest, "I think there's summat you should know."

She paused long enough for me to ask, "What?"

"I'm getting to it," she hedged. "I just don't want you to be getting yourself all upset. The thing of it is," she began again, once more carefully choosing her words, "it came to me this morning as I was getting dressed. And I thought to myself, should I make mention of it to Em, or not?"

"Make mention of what, for heaven's sake!" I responded in anxious annoyance.

"Well," she stated, "if you think back to last night, there were Daisy all dressed up nice like, in your coat and hat, and from the back looking for all the world—I mean, if I'd have been walking behind her I would have thought, right enough . . ." She began to fidget with her fingers.

"You would have thought," I stepped in to soothe her uneasiness, "that it was me. In fact," I continued on, "it's your belief that the murderer mistook Daisy for me. Am I right?"

"You knew! When?" she responded in open-mouthed amazement.

"Last night. I didn't say anything at the time for fear it would upset you even more."

"So, each of us came up with the same idea," she smiled. "Birds of a feather, that's what we are." I would have thought "great minds think alike" would have been the more appropriate analogy, but I let it pass. "There's summat else

I've been thinking about," she continued on. "A word of thanks to the Almighty wouldn't be amiss, luv. It could just have easily have been you out there 'stead of poor Daisy."

"You think I should thank Him for saving my life?"

"Well, yes, 'course I do."

"Then," I questioned, "what of Daisy?"

"How'd you mean?"

"If I'm to thank Him for sparing my life, is Daisy to curse Him from the grave for taking hers?"

"Emma Hudson," was the flustered response, "I don't know what to make of you sometimes, I don't."

"Oh, Vi," I soothed, "I'm no heretic. But it always struck me as odd that whenever we hear or read of some misfortune, a train derailment resulting in the loss of lives for example, those who are fortunate enough to have lived through it are quick to give thanks to the Creator for having spared them."

"Aye, and quite right, too," she acknowledged.

"But what," I asked, "of the men, women, children, and little babies who didn't survive? Were they so evil in God's eye that he decreed they should die? I think not. I wonder, is God's involvement in our lives as all-encompassing as we've been led to believe?"

"'Ere, now, how should I know!" was the bewildered response flung out at me from across the table. "I'm not the bleedin' pope or the archbishop of Canterbury, for that matter."

We left it at that and proceeded with the business at hand. "Now, then," I said, as we laid memo pads along with various bits of paper filled with hastily scribbled notes and sundry information out before us, "where to begin?"

"You know what they always say," smiled Vi. "When in doubt, always start—"

"At the beginning. Right. Well, then," I summarized, "we have Mr. Churchill as our client requesting we find out whether a man known only to the international police as Marcos has taken up residence in London. If so, we were to find out where he is lodged, where he goes, and who he sees. All of which," I added, affording myself a satisfied smile, "we did."

"Aye," commented my companion dryly, "and from there on in it were all downhill."

I ignored her jibe and continued on. "We are then informed by Mr. Churchill of his sojourn in South Africa as war correspondent for the *Morning Post* and, in light of that, he arranges for the *Post*'s Miles Henten to act as liaison in regard to our ongoing investigation."

"And with Mr. Churchill being captured by the Boers, and all," put in Vi, "we're stuck with this here Henten bloke."

"Who, it appears, has turned out to be a bit of a will-o'-the-wisp, I'm afraid. To continue on, another gentleman, known to us only as R, enters the picture. He meets with Marcos on two occasions that we know of, at the man's lodging and—"

"The second time at the Blue Boar. I remember that, well enough," stated Vi, most forcefully. "All that ruckus going on with poor old Paddy getting his head bashed, like."

"Poor old Paddy?" I repeated with raised eyebrows. "That's a change, isn't it? I thought you were the one who believed him to be a member of that nefarious gang."

"Well," she hedged, shifting uncomfortably in her chair, "I didn't exactly say—that is . . . Now, see here, Emma Hudson," was the now belligerent response, "it's you who's always saying everyone's a suspect 'til the culprit's caught."

"True," I agreed.

"Still, it doesn't mean a body can't have second thoughts," she meekly replied. "Off the mark, I was, with Paddy, so to speak," she reluctantly admitted, adding, "Barmy old sot that he is."

I don't know what changed her mind, and I never asked, if, in fact, she ever doubted Paddy in the first place. It may have been simply for argument's sake. With Vi, one never knew. "Well, now that we have Mr. O'Ryan back in the fold"—I smiled—"let's continue on, shall we? Going back to the night at the Blue Boar, are you sure you never saw this R chap either entering or leaving the back room with Marcos?"

"No," was the exasperated reply. "I told you, I saw nowt."

"But—"

"After I had made my way over to Paddy," she interrupted with a resigned sigh on seeing I was not about to let the matter drop so easily, "I could see him lying there holding his head with blood dripping through his fingers, like. And, oh, weren't it a nasty cut. Must have been hit with summat more than just a fist. The bloke had summat in his hand, if you ask me."

"In—his—hand," I repeated slowly, as a half-forgotten scene eased its way to the forefront of my mind. "No," I answered, "not *in* his hand . . ."

"Eh?"

"Nothing, at least, not yet. If only I knew—"

" 'Ere, what's this you're babbling on about?"

"Are you positive," I asked, ignoring her query, "that you never saw either this R chap or Marcos at all that night?"

"How could I?" she answered in no little annoyance. "I told you, whisked right by me, they did."

"Whisked right by?" I slammed my hand down on the table and literally screamed out my questions. "How tall a man was he? Color of hair? Quick! Quick!"

"Tall, he was. Light brown or blond. Oh, Em, whatever's got into you? Fair gave me a heart attack, you did!" she gasped.

"I'm sorry, Vi," I apologized. "It was just a little experiment of mine to shock you into remembering."

"Well," she answered in between gulps of air, "it did that, right enough."

I once more offered up my apologies, and, putting hand to teapot and finding it still warm, I refilled her cup and waited while she sipped her brew, bit into a biscuit, and regained her composure. "After putting me through all that, Emma Hudson," she spoke at last with a dab or two of napkin to lips, "I don't see as how it did any good. Not much of a description it was, if you ask me."

"I can't say I don't wish it could have been more," I freely admitted. "But it just might be enough. If you had remembered him as being a short, fat man, for example, I'm afraid I'd have had to set my sails in another direction."

"Well, whenever you're ready to drop anchor," was the caustic comment, "you'll let me know what you're thinking, I'm sure."

I'm afraid at that moment there was not that much I could offer her by way of explanation. "I do have a few ideas floating around," I announced. "But as yet they remain like so many numbered dots in a child's book, waiting to be connected to form the complete picture. By the way," I asked, "do you remember the story in the newspaper about the man whose body was found washed up on the banks of the Thames?"

"Yes, 'course I do," she was quick to assure me, no doubt on the assumption that had she not remembered, there'd be yet another verbal attack on her memory. "Why'd you ask?" she queried. "You don't think there's any connection with that poor dead soul and what's been going on, do you?"

"Not at first, I didn't."

"And, now?"

"Let's just say," was my noncommittal reply, "at this point in time he's yet another unconnected dot."

"Mind 'fore you go connecting all your dots," she dutifully informed me, "that there's one what leads to a ruddy bomb."

"I'm not likely to forget." I grimaced. "But,

let's leave that aside for the moment," I added, on rising from the chair.

"Where're you going now?"

"What? Oh, nowhere, I was just—"

" 'Ere, you're not going to start that pacing business, are you?" she clucked disapprovingly. "You'll have yourself a trench worn into the floor one of these days, you will."

"Oh, Vi, you know it helps me think."

" 'Bout what? If I may be so bold as to ask."

"The murder of Daisy Whyte. Now, Violet," I was quick to state, on seeing my old friend's face cloud over, "we have to be professional about this."

"What's there to think about?" was the sulky response. "We know who did her in, right enough. Marcos."

"Agreed. And we also agree," I added, in a continual retracing of my steps, "I was the intended victim. Because . . . ?" I asked, turning it back to her.

"He thought Daisy was you. That's plain enough," she stated, rising to gather up what dishes remained on the table. "Well, I have to do summat," she explained without my asking. "If you think I can just sit here while you carry on traipsin' back and forth in front of me like some caged animal—"

"Oh, alright," I acquiesced, once more taking my place opposite her at the table. "But, don't you see what we're overlooking?"

"No, but I'm sure you'll tell me."

"The question is, what made Marcos believe it was me he saw walking down Baker Street last night?"

"Eh?"

I tried again. "How did he know, or thought he knew, it was me? Lord knows we've never been introduced," I added facetiously. "As far as we know, he isn't even aware I exist."

"Now I see what you're saying," she answered with an understanding nod of the head. "Here we are being all secretive, like, and he shows up nice as you please outside the door, so to speak, ready to do you in. Fair gives me the willies, it does."

"I'd rather have answers than willies."

"Well, it's easy enough to figure out, ain't it," she stated all too smugly. "He saw you following him when he was meandering 'bout town, then, without you knowing it, he followed you."

"Doubled back, you mean?"

"Aye, that's what they call it, doubled back."

"That, of course," I conceded, "is one answer."

"Have another, do you?"

"Hmmm," I answered, returning to the notes at hand. "Our main concern," I announced, while continuing to scan through the material, "is to find out where the bombing is to take place."

"Maybe it's time to see that inspector bloke from Scotland Yard what knows Mr. Holmes."

"Lestrade?"

"Aye. Let him know what's been going on."

I could see how, at first light, it would seem obvious to Vi that the best idea, at this point in time, would be to bring the Yard into it. But, as I reminded her, bring them into what? "Inspector Lestrade," said I, as if addressing the man himself, "I'm here to inform you that the international terrorist, known only as Marcos, is now residing within the city of London." "Where, in London, would he be, Mrs. Hudson?" I asked, dropping my voice a register or two, in taking on the role of the inspector. "I don't know, I'm afraid. But he plans to blow up a house." "A house, you say? And where would this house be?" "That, I don't know either. Although, I might also mention I believe him to be responsible for the murder of one Daisy Whyte." "And what proof do you have for making such an allegation, Mrs. Hudson?" "None at all, Inspector."

"Alright, alright, Sarah Bernhardt." Vi laughed. "You don't have to put on a three-act play, I get your point. Still, all in all—"

"What," I asked. "Still uncertain?"

"It's just that, I mean, what with it being a bomb, and all—Do you think," she asked a trifle apprehensively, "we should see if his Nibs might have an idea or two?"

"Ask Mr. Holmes? Certainly not!" I snapped. "This is our case and solve it we shall, m'girl." Though to be perfectly frank, I don't know who I was trying to convince more with my outburst, myself or my companion. I did, however, have one consolation, in that while I had no idea where the bombing would occur, there were bits and pieces of the picture that were slowly settling themselves into place.

"Right, then. If you're not interested in Mr. Holmes's help, that's all very well, I'm sure," was the snippy reply. " 'Course, half of London could be blown up at any minute now and us along with it, like as not."

"Then we'd better put our thinking caps on, hadn't we?" I smiled sweetly. "Ah, here it is."

"What?"

"A list I wrote down of the places that Marcos took in when we had him under surveillance."

"Fat lot of good that'll do. Nowt but typical tourist sights, they were. And some down in Soho that weren't so typical, if you know what I mean."

"Here's something we didn't pick up on," I announced, running my finger down the page. "Aside from the music halls, pubs, shops, galleries, and whatnot, the one place we trailed him to on more than one occasion was the Parliament buildings. Look at the number of times you followed him there as well as me and Paddy," I said, extending the paper over to her.

"I don't know what he was so interested in," she announced, with a cursory glance at the page. "He only sat in the visitors' gallery for no more than fifteen minutes, at best, each time."

"True, in my case, as well," I added. "As far as I could tell he had little or no interest in any of the political debates being carried out on the floor below. By the by, there's something else I should mention," I added. "I've a confession to make, actually."

"Oh, aye?"

"On those occasions when I had trailed him to the visitors' gallery, he had the uncanny knack of disappearing on me after sitting no more than ten or fifteen minutes." That being said, I fully expected a snide remark or two from across the table on my abilities or lack of them in letting him slip away. I was pleasantly relieved, if not surprised, when she announced, "Same thing happened to me, it did. I'd be sitting up there in that crowd, trying to keep me eye on him when, 'fore you know it, he was gone."

"There's something strange about it all," I stated, rising from the chair only to return to it lest I again vex Violet with additional pacing. "We have Marcos entering the building, going up to the gallery, staying but a short while, then slipping out unnoticed by either you or me and, Paddy as well, I would imagine. What if," I beamed, with an inspired thought, "the prime minister is the target? Marcos takes his place in the gallery with the idea of checking out the PM: in effect, taking in the measure of the man who is to be his next victim."

"So, what you're saying is, you think it's 10 Downing Street Marcos is getting set to blow up, is that it?"

Her question completely deflated me. "No, it can't be." I groaned in the realization of my error. "With the prime minister's residence located on Downing, it could hardly qualify as being on the Thames."

"Never mind, luv, it were a good idea while it lasted," announced my companion with a halfhearted smile.

"In any event," I added, "as I recall, the prime minister was never actually in attendance anytime I was there. Pity, not having the opportunity of seeing him. You?"

"Aye, it were the same with me. As far as I remember, he never was in the House those times I'd be there trying to keep an eye on—"

"What did you say?" I blurted out.

"Eh? I just said, it were the same with—"

"No, not that," I cut in again, being barely able to control my excitement. "You said, he was never in the—"

"House!" we jubilantly chorused.

"Of course, that's it—the house on the Thames as Marcos called it, is in reality," I exclaimed, "the House of Commons!" I sank back in my chair with a feeling that a great weight had been lifted off me.

"The house on Thames go boom." Violet spat the words out in disgust. "If he spoke proper English like the rest of us, we'd not have been flummoxed."

"Be that as it may, we now at long last know the location." I beamed. "And it proves I was right about the prime minister being the target—he *has* to be!"

"He'll be happy to hear that, I'm sure. 'Ere," she continued, after receiving a wry smile from yours truly, "didn't we read something in the papers recently 'bout him being laid up with influenza?"

"Yes, that's right," I acknowledged. "I'd forgotten that." I paused for a moment or two before ending my thought with a dramatic snap of my fingers. "And that, m'girl," I announced, feeling quite pleased with myself, "has been, and is, the reason for all the delay. Marcos enters the gallery, sits there long enough to realize it is to be yet another day without the prime minister in attendance, and leaves. He can't commit the deed if his victim's not there."

"And what's he going to do when the PM does show up, eh?" questioned a now skeptical Violet. "Throw a bomb over the ruddy railing? He'd be chucked over himself quick enough, and no mistake."

"I don't have all the answers," I protested, pausing as I rose midway off my chair.

"Oh, pace away if you've a mind to," sighed Vi, as I stood hovering between a standing/sitting position.

And pace away I did, until at last announcing, "No, not the railing."

"Eh?"

"The bomb won't come from above, but below. Yes," I continued, expressing my thoughts aloud, "that would also explain his disappearing act."

"Clear as mud, you are."

"When you lost sight of him, what did you do?" I asked, while just as quickly supplying the answer. "If you were like me, you scoured corridors, staircases, and the steps outside, right?"

"Aye. Right, enough."

"Then if he was never seen leaving the building, it stands to reason—"

"He were still inside!" she exclaimed with a smug smile of satisfaction that just as abruptly soured into puzzlement. "But where did he go?"

"Let's go back a bit. As you say, he's not about to chuck a bomb over the railing. The man values his life more than that. He may be a terrorist, but he's not a fanatic. But," I added, with a tapping of finger to table for emphasis, "if he were to set a bomb off *underneath* the floor of the Commons—"

"He'd wipe out the PM and half his cabinet!" she gasped.

To actually hear the deed being spoken of aloud was both a horrifying and sobering moment for the two of us, with Violet at last breaking the silence with a somber, "That's a bit much, ain't it?"

"To say the least," I sadly agreed. "But remember there's a war being waged, where rules of conduct and codes of honor are becoming as obsolete as plumed helmets. As to his disappearance," I continued, "I think it's safe to assume he makes his way down to the bowels of the building searching for the exact location where the bomb is to be planted for maximum effect. He must also take into consideration the amount of time involved for both his arrival and departure. His route of escape, if you will."

"Then, you actually think," spoke my companion as the realization of the magnitude of the crime became more apparent, "that he'd really—'Ere," was the sudden and angry outburst, "who's he think he is, eh? Guy Fawkes?" referring to that seventeenth-century conspirator and his infamous Gunpowder Plot to blow up Parliament.

"History does have a way of repeating itself," I reflected. "Still, it's our job to see that Marcos is as unsuccessful as was his more famous Jacobean counterpart."

"Hanging's too good for him," she said.

"We have to catch him first," I said.

TEN

Body and Soul

So caught up was I in the excitement of knowing what we had been able to piece together, I felt completely rejuvenated and more determined than ever to see it through to the end. My hypothesis of what I believed had transpired seemed so right. It had all fallen into place, as it were. Still, I was not gullible enough to think it was so simply because I believed it to be. The operative word was, as I mentioned, hypothesis. And it would remain just that if we continued to do nothing more than sit at home congratulating ourselves. Nor had I forgotten that there remained a plethora of as yet unanswered questions.

Where was Marcos at that very minute? Sitting in the gallery hoping for an appearance by the prime minister? Would this, in fact, be the day the PM—Lord Salisbury, that is—showed up? Was he there already? If so, was Marcos, even now, engaged in his devilish business somewhere within the basement of that august building? All these questions and more I put to my old friend and companion.

"I wish I had the answers for you, luv," replied Violet with a heavy sigh of despair. "One good thing about it all, though," she added on a brighter note, "if Salisbury's not there today, Marcos will be taking off for good. Leastways, that's what he told that R bloke, according to what Paddy heard."

"But if the PM does show up and we've done nothing . . ."

"Aye, I know what you mean."

More pacing. "If only we had a crystal ball," I remarked, partly in jest if not frustration, "to see at this very minute what *is* taking place in the House of Commons. Then, again," I said, stopping dead in my tracks to face Vi head-on, "we don't really need a crystal ball, do we?" My question was not given without a feeling of trepidation as to what her reaction would be.

After a moment or two, as the meaning of my words became apparent to her, she exclaimed, " 'Ere, I know what you're thinking, Emma Hudson, and I'll have none of it."

I was, of course, making reference to her ability on being able to induce an out-of-body experience at will. On a previous case, when she had consented to release her spiritual self from her physical body to surreptitiously gain much-needed information, she had proved to be most helpful indeed. But it was not a request I asked lightly. She was not a young woman, and the strain it could impose on her if the "journey" was of a lengthy duration could, I feared, result in dire consequences. But we were caught in a bind, and time was of the essence. We simply had to know what was taking place within the House before we could make our move. All this I put to my companion, adding that the first hint of a "tugging" (the sensation of her ethereal self seeking a return to its more solid body) would be a signal for her teleporting travels to cease immediately.

"Oh, I see," she said. "Now I'm to go gliding off over the rooftops of London, am I, like I was Father Christmas, is that it?"

Although her response was steeped in sarcasm, I believed she was secretly intrigued by the idea. "Well, actually, yes," I answered. "If you could then glide over, as you say, to the House of Commons to 'see' whether the PM or Marcos were there, it—"

"Right. Anything else, then? Perhaps I could drop by Buck House for a cuppa with the Widow of Windsor, while I'm at it."

I could see she was determined to have me coax, cajole, and plead with her in order to puff up her own importance. I took the opposite tack. "Well, of course, dear, if you'd rather not."

"'Ere, now, I didn't say I wouldn't, did I?" she grumbled, adding, "It's just that I don't know how long I can stay 'out,' like."

"As soon as you feel it's too taxing, just say the word," I answered, with a reassuring pat to her arm.

We made our way into the parlor and, as Violet eased herself out full-length on the chesterfield, I took the opportunity of placing a cushion under her head before bringing a chair up alongside.

As to the validity of whether one in a meditative state can release the spiritual from the physical self, in effect creating an out-of-body experience, I make no judgement one way or the other. Nor do I seek belief from any who may read these lines. I can but set down what I was witness to and ask of those who view the world of the supernatural through unbelieving eyes to keep an open mind.

As Vi has described it to me, she lies perfectly still, letting her mind clear itself of its myriad thoughts, until she at last succumbs to a semi-conscious state of being. At which point a tingling and/or numbing sensation, starting at the feet, gradually envelops the entire body. The room itself, now "seen" through closed eyelids, is basked in a soft golden hue. As the glow begins to fade, Violet is left with a sense of occupying two bodies—physical and spiritual. The vaporous soul then floats out and up as effortlessly as would a plume of smoke from a chimney.

I continued to sit and watch her deep rhythmic breathing for no more than a minute or so before the words "I'm out" were voiced in a barely audible monotone.

"Are you in this room?" I asked, though seeing her lying there before me, I must admit the question did seem a little foolish. And yet. . . .

"Outside. Floating just above Baker Street," she answered with little or no emotion to the voice, adding, "Starting to rain, it is."

"Are you wet?" I asked, not knowing quite what else to say.

"I don't feel wet. I don't feel nothing, really. Queer, ain't it? I—oh!"

"What is it? What's the matter?" I cried out in alarm.

"Oh, Em," came the reply, accompanied by heavy breathing, "I feel myself being whisked along ever so fast. Everything is a blur."

As this was the first time I had actually "sat in" on one of her spiritual sojourns, I was becoming quite frightened, to say the least. "Perhaps it's best," I said, trying to control the quiver in my voice, "if we call the whole thing off. If you were to get 'lost' out there—"

"Don't fret, luv," she answered with a smile as the slightly slurred voice droned on, "I'll be alright. I just have to think where I want to go and, 'fore you know it, I'm there."

"Can you make out anything down below?" I questioned, while trying to visualize the scene being played out behind those closed eyelids. "London Bridge? The Tower? The—"

"I'm there."

"What? Where?"

"The House."

"You're—So soon? Where, exactly?" I asked, with hands clenching and unclenching in nervous tension. "The visitors' gallery?"

A deep sigh. "I am now."

"And Marcos," I stammered. "Can you see Marcos?"

"Aye, now I can." She made a face. "Sitting right in front, he is. Leaning over. Elbows resting on the rail."

I was almost afraid to ask the next question, but ask it, I did. "Do you see Lord Salisbury?" I held my breath while watching the movement of pupils dart back and forth under the closed eyelids.

"That'd be his seat down there in the front row, would it?"

"Yes," I answered. "It would be to the right of the Speaker."

"The what?"

"The Speaker of the House," I explained. "That's the gentleman seated on the raised dais facing both parties."

"No," she answered after a pause, "the seat's empty. He's not there."

I sank back in my chair and breathed a satisfied sigh of relief. There'd be no bombing today, or any other day, I told myself. With the PM once more absent, Marcos would no doubt be on the first ship out before nightfall. It was at that point I was about to request my companion make her "return" when she suddenly announced, "Some toff on the other side just stood up. Sayin' summat 'bout the PM, he is."

"Oh, yes?" was my mildly uninterested reply. "And what would that be?"

" 'Mr. Speaker,' he's saying, 'I was wondering if perhaps the deputy prime minister would be so kind as to inform the House as to when we can expect the pleasure of Lord Salisbury's company on the floor. As you know, Mr. Speaker,' he goes on, all hoity-toity, like, 'we've been given to believe he's been suffering from an illness of late. Boer-War-itus, I believe it's called.' Oh, Em, you should hear the laughter, least on one side of the House. Boos and cat-calls, on the other." Her face soured in disgust. "Like schoolchildren they are, the lot of 'em."

"I've often heard them referred to as such," I remarked with a wry smile.

"Now the other one's standing up."

"The deputy prime minister?"

"I suppose."

I thought it was now time to "call her back," as it were, but as she was so caught up in what she was "seeing," and as there was no longer any threat of a bombing, I let her ramble on.

" 'Mr. Speaker,' he says," she continued, " 'I would like to assure the honorable gentleman across the aisle that Her Majesty's government has no apologies to make for its policies regarding the war now being fought so gallantly by Her Majesty's forces in South Africa. As to the prime minister, Mr. Speaker, I'm sure the House will join me in wishing him a speedy—' "

For some unknown reason she immediately stopped short.

"What's up?" I asked.

"Some little tyke just handed him a note," she answered.

"A page?"

"I said," repeated Vi in some annoyance, "a note."

"No," I explained, "the boy's called a page. He delivers messages to—oh, let it go." I smiled.

As I continued to sit watching over her, I noted that other than being pale of face, she appeared relaxed, and, except for the outstretched arms that lay alongside her body with hands palms up, Violet appeared quite normal—or as normal as anyone could under the circumstances. If Mr. Holmes had taken it upon himself to eavesdrop outside the parlor door, whatever would he have thought, I wonder, for my companion's astral abilities were a secret shared only twixt us two.

"He's read the note and stuck it in his fob pocket," spoke Vi, as she began once more to relay the scene as it unfolded before her.

"Are you sure they can't see you?" I asked.

" 'Course not," was the irritated reply. "Can't even see meself, if it comes to that."

I shook my head in complete bewilderment. There are more things in heaven and earth . . .

"Got a big smile on his face now, he has," continued Vi. " 'Mr. Speaker,' he's saying, 'I've just been informed that Lord Salisbury has just entered the building and should be joining us here on the floor shortly.' "

I literally leaped from my chair. How quickly everything had changed for the worse. The man could be walking into certain death; and how many of his colleagues would be taken with him should an explosion occur? And I had no doubt it would if something wasn't done immediately. But what? I eased a now trembling body once more back into my chair as visions of carnage, confusion, hysteria, and bloodied bodies swept over me.

"Vi," I asked, trying to keep my emotions in check, "what's Marcos doing? Is he still there?"

"Should—come—back—now." The words

were forced, the voice tired, and the breathing labored.

"Oh, no!" I moaned inwardly in despair. "Not now, of all times." Whatever that invisible force is that signals a return to the physical self, it was now making itself felt within the mirrored image of her ethereal being. While the consequences of ignoring the warnings of this spiritual umbilical cord would, at best, be speculative, heart failure, brain damage, and even death itself could not be ruled out.

"Marcos, you say?" the voice droned out. "I'll try."

"No, Vi!" I cried out most emphatically. "It's not worth it. It's time you brought yourself back."

"I'll be alright," she assured me with a wisp of a smile on that sleeplike face. A pause, then, "He's getting up. Looks like he's getting ready to leave."

My heart sank. He was about to make his move. There was no way to make it over there on time.

"Wait."

"What?"

"He's sitting back down—folding his arms, like—just sitting there."

At last I was able to afford myself a small sigh of relief. Marcos had given me what I most needed—time. "Quick, Vi," I pleaded, on noting the voice had faded into a whisper, "you must come back, now!"

"Right you are, luv," was the barely audible reply.

After taking a deep breath, followed by a

slow exhalation of air, her body suddenly gave
an involuntary jerk as if hit by an electrical
force. The eyelids, like fluttering butterfly
wings, flickered spasmodically as a now
healthly glow seeped into the skin. After slowly
orienting herself to the more familiar surroundings of the room, she assumed a sitting position
and, with a final rub or two to the eyes, asked,
"How'd I do?"

"Splendidly!" I cried with a warm embrace
to a now fully awake and alert Violet. And
splendid it was. A tour de force in astral pro-
jection that to this day leaves me with a bewil-
dering sense of awe as to what the human mind
is capable of; and, though at one time I had
thoughts of trumpeting the news of my companion's out-of-body experiences to press and
public alike, in retrospect, I believe I made the
right decision in forgoing any such disclosure.
It had not been that many years ago when a
certain Mr. Darwin and his theories on evolu-
tion set off a storm that continues to this very
day. Neither Violet nor I had any wish to become embroiled in any such similar contro-
versy.

"What do you think Marcos is up to?" asked
Vi. "Just sitting there nice as you please, he is."

"It's my guess he's waiting to see if the prime
minister is actually going to show up."

"But he heard what—oh, I see what you're
saying," she acknowledged with a knowing
smile.

"He may be a terrorist with murder in his
heart," I stated, returning the smile, "but he's
not unlike a great many of us in one respect."

"He don't trust politicians, right?"

"Exactly. A point in our favor. It gives us time, though very little I grant you," I announced while in the process of eyeing her up and down.

" 'Ere," she sputtered, "what's all this fisheye business you're giving me, eh?"

"You do feel alright now, do you?"

" 'Course I do. Tough as old boots, I am. Why'd you ask?"

She certainly appeared to be the picture of health, but considering what she had been through, I was still a little hesitant in asking, "Do you feel up to doing a little bit more traveling?"

She eyed me warily.

"In the normal way this time," I hastened to inform her with a reassuring smile.

"Oh, well, that's different then, isn't it? Had me worried for a bit, you did."

"Then, c'mon, old girl," I announced with a sense of urgency on rising to a standing position. "It's time we made our move."

ELEVEN

We're on Our Way

∽ AS WE APPROACHED the hall closet Vi thought to ask what intentions I had with regard to the coat and hat I had lent to Daisy. I answered that I hadn't really thought about it but, in any event, I had no intentions of collecting it from her effects, knowing I could never wear it again but that it would bring back too many unpleasant memories not only of her demise but of a night best left forgotten.

"Well, then," spoke my companion, deftly turning the conversation in another direction, "I suppose we're off to Parliament then, are we?"

"I'm afraid," I informed her, while knowing only too well what her reaction would be, "that I'm going to have to make that trip alone."

"You're what!" came the not unexpected vitriolic outburst.

"Don't worry," I hastened to assure her, "I've a very important errand for you as well. Two, actually. One, to Scotland Yard, for if ever there was a need to bring Inspector Lestrade into this, that time is now. And, second," I continued, as we each assisted the other into our respective coats, "I'd like you to hightail it over to the offices of the *Morning Post*."

"Well, yes, Scotland Yard, I can see," she acknowledged while in the act of inserting pin into hat and hair. "But what's this with the *Post*? I'm to see that Henten bloke, is that it?"

"I doubt very much if you'll find Mr. Henten there," I answered as I set about buttoning up my gloves. "No, you're to see a Mr. Farnsworth. Mention my name and ask if he'd be so kind as to describe Mr. Henten to you. One more thing, and this is important," I added. "Find out if he has a mole on his cheek."

"Who, Farnsworth?"

"No! For heaven's sake, Violet," I snapped. "Henten. Miles Henten."

"Well, there's no need to get all snippy, like. And anyway, what's all this business about a mole, eh? You've seen the ruddy begger often enough to know whether—"

"Sorry, Vi," I cut in. "I wish I had time to explain, but we *are* in a hurry. Now, as to the inspector," I stated with my hand now resting on the doorknob, "you must convince him of the urgency in getting over to Parliament as quickly as possible. Tell him it could be—no, tell him it *is* a matter of life and death."

"Aye, don't worry, I'll see to it right enough. Only, are you sure you should go there on your own? Might be best, Em," she advised, "to wait 'til the inspector shows up."

"Would that I could. But we're running out of time even as we speak. I've no other choice."

"True enough, I suppose," came the reply in conjunction with a heavy, heartfelt sigh.

Something was troubling her. "What is it, Vi?" I asked, on noting a trembling lip.

"You take care of yourself, Emma Hudson."

God bless her. A matter of life and death I had said. Yes, it was quite possible I could end up among the death toll should the horror of what we feared became a reality. But I felt it was something I could not, would not, let myself dwell upon. And so it was, after a silent exchange of hugs coupled with good-luck wishes, we were now ready to set off on our respective journeys.

I flung open the door.

"Ah, Mrs. Hudson, Mrs. Warner, is it coming or going, you are?" came the greeting as we were about to step out into a steady drizzle of rain.

"Paddy O'Ryan!" we exclaimed in surprise, with Vi adding, "And what have you been up to, eh?"

"And what haven't I been up to, Mrs. Warner? That'd be the question. Faith, 'tis a tale you two ladies would not be believing."

"Aye, I've no doubt you're right on that score," commented Vi. "But we've no time for your tales today, m'lad."

The man appeared crestfallen. "Would you be having any news yourselves, then?" he asked.

"More than we can tell you about right now," I answered, as Vi and I descended onto the walk with umbrellas unfurled. "And for pity's sake, Paddy O'Ryan," I went on, taking in the bedraggled figure before me, "get under the brolly. You look like a wet puppy."

"It's that thoughtful you are, Mrs. Hudson." He smiled, edging his way in beside me. "And would it be out of place in asking where it is you're going?"

"Em," cried Vi, before an answer could be given, "we're in luck! There's a cab what's just pulled up across the street and one's coming round the corner. Oy, cabbie!" she sang out.

"I'll make for the one opposite us," I replied.

"Right you are. Good luck then, and be careful, luv." She waved, as I took off across the street with the little man still trailing beside me.

As I stepped up and into the cab, with an assist from Paddy, I at last had the opportunity to answer him as to my destination and, to question him as to whether he wished to accompany me. On readily receiving an affirmative reply, I beckoned him in, and, with the crack of the cabby's whip whistling through the air, we took off at a good trot down Baker Street.

Above the clatter of iron shoes on cobbled stone, I was able to give him, at best, a digested summary of the events as they now stood, while, needless to say, omitting any reference to Violet's astral visitation to the House of Commons. I also sought to impress upon him the possible dangers that lay ahead. I put it to him he could, if he so desired, take his leave at the next corner, and no more would be said or thought of it.

"What's this you're sayin', now!" he cried out in a shocked, if not indignant, tone. "Leave you alone to do battle with this Marcos creature, is that it? And haven't I a score to settle with him, meself?"

"I take it that means you've decided to come along." I smiled. And while it may appear I made light of his company, Lord knows I'm no hero and was more than grateful for his presence and any assistance he might be able to render.

As we continued to traverse the rain-splashed streets, my thoughts turned to Violet. Would she, I wondered, be able to convince Inspector Lestrade of the gravity of the situation as it now stood? And, what of Farnsworth? Information she would be able to obtain from him would prove invaluable, should his answers coincide with my suppositions. It was at a somewhat later time that I was to learn in detail from my companion the outcome of her visits to Messrs Lestrade and Farnsworth, the account of which I now relate.

On arriving at that Gothic-like edifice known as Scotland Yard and requesting to see Inspector Lestrade, Vi was directed up a flight of stairs, down a corridor, and around a corner before at last coming to a windowless door bearing the nameplate of the good inspector. Finding it slightly ajar, she rapped but once before poking her head round for a look-see.

"Inspector Lestrade," she called out, on seeing the man hunched over his desk while in the process of riffling through a sheaf of papers, "got a minute, have you?"

Somewhat startled, he made a motion of half-rising from his chair before announcing, "I know you. You're Mrs.—ah?"

"Warner."

"Yes, that's right," he answered with a nod of the head and a beckoning of the hand. "Come in, come in. You're a friend of Mrs.—ah?"

"Hudson. Mrs. Emma Hudson, what boards Mr. Sherlock Holmes and Dr. Watson."

"Yes, of course," he acknowledged. "I believe we've met at the Baker Street household on those times when I had occasion to call upon Mr. Holmes."

"That's right. Sharp as a tack, you are," cooed Violet, who knew the value of placing flattery before a request.

"That's the ticket one needs in this business," he stated, affording himself a self-indulgent smile while motioning Vi to a seat before the desk. "A razor-sharp memory. Wouldn't be where I am today without it. Now then," he asked, leaning back in his chair with hands firmly clasped to lapels, "what can I do for you, Mrs.—ah?"

"Warner," repeated Violet, hiding her annoyance behind a forced smile while taking in the measure of the man Dr. Watson had once described as a sallow, rat-faced individual. And while I would not have put it so bluntly, the beak nose, beady eyes, prominent cheekbones, and tapering chin did, to some extent, present a face not unlike that of the species Rodentia. Still, I had always found him to be a fair man if, at times, overly pompous, as are such men

who have obtained a limited degree of authority on rising up from the ranks.

"Yes, well, it's about this Marcos bloke," began Vi, only to be stopped short by a startled
outburst from across the desk.

"Marcos! What would you know of Marcos!"
he bellowed. "That information is of a private
nature."

"Aye, well, be that as it may be," she blithely
replied. "We only know, Mrs. Hudson and me,
that is, that he's about to blow up Parliament,
like. So you'd best get a move on."

As Vi tells it, she thought the poor man was
about to go into a state of shock. "Blow up Parliament! Blow up Parliament! I warn you, madam," he spluttered, "if this is some kind of a
joke Mr. Holmes is playing at—"

"He knows nowt about it," protested Violet.
"Found out about it ourselves, we did. You
see," she continued on, trying to put it all into
perspective, and from the inspector's stand-
point, failing miserably, "Mrs. Hudson and I
are private detectives ourselves, you might
say."

"Private—you and—good God!" The little
man shook his head in complete bewilderment.
"Is there something about the Baker Street
house that breeds detectives like rabbits?" He
set aside any reply Vi could have made with an
airy wave of his hand before pausing but a moment to regroup his thoughts. Edging forward
in his chair, Lestrade studied my companion for
the longest minute, wondering, no doubt, if the
woman opposite was indeed speaking the truth
or was, at best, completely mad. "You say Mar-

cos is about to blow up Parliament," he spoke at last, "by that, I take it, you mean he intends to use some kind of delay device in setting off the charge?"

"Oh, I wouldn't know anything 'bout that, only—"

"That he intends to blow up Parliament," he added, dryly. "And you say Sherlock Holmes knows nothing of this?" he again questioned, knowing that Mr. Holmes, while not a humorless man was, like most men of serious mien, not above perpetrating a practical joke, more often than not at his or Dr. Watson's expense.

"No, I told you, he ain't involved in it at all."

"Then what proof do you have," he asked as the two beady brown eyes burrowed into her, "that what you say is true?"

"Proof? Well," answered my tart-tongued friend, "we could sit here and listen to it go off. Would that be proof enough for you?"

"Now, see here, my good woman," he snapped, "questions have to be asked and answers given. Play it by the book, that's the ticket in this business. Not like some so-called detective I could mention who is continually running off in all directions testing out new ideas and theories. No, madam," he assured her, "imagination will never replace rules and regulations." Thus, having dutifully espoused his approval of maintaining the status quo of present-day criminology, he continued. "Now, then, you say you and Mrs.—ah?"

"Hudson."

"Quite. You say, you are private detectives. Then, no doubt you are engaged by someone."

"Aye."

"Who is—?"

"Well," hedged Vi, "I don't know if it's proper, like, to tell, but I suppose under the circumstances . . ."

"Yes?"

"Mr. Winston Churchill."

His reaction was one of stunned silence. A silence that was at last broken by his crying out the singular word: "Royce!"

An adjoining door was immediately flung open as in stepped the aforementioned Royce.

"Who's the best man when it comes to explosives, Sergeant?"

"Explosives? That'd be Jenkins, sir."

"Right, then. Tell him to put a crew together and report to me on the double."

The sergeant hesitated long enough, with eyes darting back and forth between my companion and his superior to ask, "Is the Yard in any danger of—?"

"Now, Royce!" barked Lestrade.

"Well, I'm that relieved you believe me at last," spoke Violet, as the sergeant beat a hasty retreat out the door.

"Believe you, madam? Believe you? Why shouldn't I believe you?" was the mocking response. "After all, you wander into my office, sit yourself down and tell me that an international terrorist plans to set off a bomb in the House of Commons. And how do you know all this?" he continued on in like manner. "Because you and Sherlock Holmes's landlady are private detectives who have for a client, Winston Churchill, the hero of the day to press and public alike. And who, if I'm not mistaken, now resides in a prisoner-of-war camp in South Africa."

"Right you are, on all counts," smiled Violet sweetly, thereby infuriating the good inspector even more.

"My dear Mrs.—ah?"

"Warner," Vi wearily repeated for the umpteenth time.

"Quite. My dear Mrs. Warner, what you may, or may not understand," she was duly informed in icy tones, "is that I believe you because I don't know of a single soul on God's green earth who could have made up such an incredible story!"

Whatever his reasoning, Violet, it seemed, had in her own way succeeded in bringing Scotland Yard on board. Before taking her leave she related in detail, as best she could, all pertinent information as to where and when we believed the bombing would occur, adding, "Mind you see nothing happens to Mrs. Hudson." Then, after a pause, "And yourself as well, Inspector—ah?"

"Lestrade, madam. Lestrade."

"Quite," she answered, suppressing a smug little smile.

As with the inspector, I was also to learn later from my companion that her encounter with Mr. Farnsworth of the *Morning Post* had proceeded along much smoother lines and, that she was able to glean from that venerable gentleman, answers to those questions I had asked to be put forward. With her mission now successfully completed she once more hailed a cabbie with orders that he take her straightaway at a good gallop to the houses of Parliament.

As for Paddy and me, as our cab continued to round this corner and that at a most frightening pace, I thought back to the little Irishman's earlier statement about "a tale we wouldn't be believing." To smooth out any feathers Vi and I might have ruffled by our brushing aside his report as being, at best, inconsequential and, in truth, with the belief his chatter would help take my mind off what lay ahead, I bade him tell his story. As he did, I sat, for the most part, in both openmouthed amazement and shamefaced embarrassment for having exhibited a certain indifference when first he spoke of it; for a most harrowing tale it was.

According to Paddy, on the previous afternoon he had taken himself down to Shandling's, that murky dwelling of a lodging house where, in what now seems like ages ago, we had first met. It was while thus boisterously engaged, to quote Paddy, "in the bending of an elbow or two" round a lager-filled table with his mates that he was more than a little surprised, to say the least, on seeing none other than Marcos enter the establishment, jostle his way through a group of workingmen at the bar, and make straightaway for the stairs, leaving my little Irish friend with the realization that after the man's disappearance from his Tench Street digs he had obviously taken new lodgings for himself at Shandling's.

Whether it was Dutch courage brought about

by an inordinate consumption of spirits or just plain Irish foolhardiness, he decided to follow him up the stairs, where, on reaching the landing, he was just in time to see Marcos enter his room. Having discovered where he was now lodged and the room he occupied, he needn't have troubled himself any farther. But our Mr. O'Ryan took it upon himself to listen outside the door, for whatever reason Lord only knows. In any event, it turned out to be his first mistake.

No sooner had he pressed himself against the paneling than the door was immediately flung open inwardly with such unexpected suddenness that Paddy found himself, on stumbling into the room, being grabbed unceremoniously by seat of pants and scruff of neck and hurled to the floor.

"You think I don't know you followed me?" The voice was mockingly cruel, the fists clenched. "You think maybe Marcos stupid?"

Sprawled in rag-doll fashion on the floor, Paddy only half heard the voice from above as that stout heart now beat with such an intensity he thought his eardrums would burst.

"You smell funny, wharf rat. Who are you? Who you work for?" The questions received added emphasis by a sharp kick to those spindly legs.

"It's a dockhand, I am." The words came in short gasps as he gulped in air. "Whenever it is I can be finding the work," he added, to the towering figure looming over him.

An eerie silence followed, with Marcos quietly studying his captive until a bushy black eyebrow above those deep-set eyes was raised in recognition. "I know you," he announced at last. "You fellah at Blue Boar."

"The Blue Boar, is it you're saying?" spoke Paddy, rising to the occasion, if not from the floor, by the spreading of a little Irish blarney. "And aren't I always being told I look like someone else? No, it wouldn't be me you'd be thinking of. Not at all, at all."

"I think you lie, wharf rat," the man replied, crossing the room to where a bottle of gin lay waiting on a small round table by the bed.

With the man's back to him, the little Irishman, seeing his chance, bounded up and across the room for the door he now found himself unable to open. In a state of fear and confusion he continued to push against it until remembered only too late it opened inward. As a hand clamped down on his shoulder, he was spun around and forcefully thrust across the room into a chair. Cord was produced from a drawer and within seconds arms were secured behind the rung-back chair, and ankles bound to its wooden staves. Having thus secured his intruder, Marcos awarded himself a double shot of gin before extending the bottled contents in tantalizing fashion under the little Irishman's nose. "You want drink?" he asked, innocently enough.

"Ah," came the sigh, "it's that kind you are, sir. If you could be but untying me arms . . . ?"

"Sure, I untie you. I give you all the drink you want," announced the man in hearty manner, as would a host to a favored guest.

"You'd be doin' that for me now, would

you?" queried a puzzled Paddy, unsure as to the why of this sudden change in demeanor but thankful for it nonetheless.

"As soon as I get truth from you," came the reply, with a wisp of a smile beneath the moustache as the bottle continued to be swung in pendulum-like precision before him. "You have all of it. See—nearly full."

I can't win for losing thought our Mr. O'Ryan, knowing that whether he continued to lie or speak the truth, the end result would be the same. He'd never leave the room alive. He could do nothing but continue to state his "innocence" and bide his time in the hope of— what? He didn't know. "But, I'm tellin' you, I'd not be the man you think I am," he sang out with as much sincerity as he could muster.

Obviously, it wasn't enough. The muscles in his captor's face and neck tightened in controlled rage as an arm was swung menacingly upward; but before the blow could be struck a sharp staccato rapping at the door broke the air like so many pistol shots. The arm returned to its side. Again the sound of two long raps, then three in rapid succession, was heard. Marcos strode over and opened the door for his new arrival.

"Could you see who he was?" I asked of Paddy, as we continued to be jostled about within the cab.

"Not a bit of him," I was informed. "With the chair facing the window, me back was to whoever it was that entered. But I know it was that R fellah from the night at the Blue Boar," he added. "There'd be no doubtin' that."

"Why, so?"

"From what it was they were saying," he replied, continuing with his tale.

"I say, what's all this about?" questioned the man.

"A little wharf rat I catch crawling round my door," answered Marcos. "I think he come spying."

"Spying?" repeated the man with no little amusement. "That old sot, a spy? I say, old man, I doubt if Her Majesty's government is that hard-up for recruits. A wharf rat you called him and a wharf rat he is. Get ahold of yourself, my dear Marcos. I think your nerves are getting the best of you."

"You, think. I don't think—Marcos know! He was at Blue Boar night of meeting. You hit him outside door."

"Did I, indeed? I hit somebody, as I recall. What's he got to say to all this?"

"It's innocent I am, Your Worship!" cried out Paddy, while attempting to crane his neck around for a view of the man behind him.

"There you are, you see. He say's he's innocent. I say, that gin looks awfully inviting."

"Pour, yourself."

"Thanks."

"Everything big joke to you. No joke to Marcos." The voice was clearly agitated. "I take all the risks."

The other man gulped his drink and set the glass down before replying in a more conciliatory tone. "The thing is, my dear Marcos, I know his lot. Found him outside your door, you say? No doubt looking to see what he could nick from your room. Steal the pennies off a dead man's eyes, his kind would, and think tuppence of it. A common thief at best, old man, but hardly a spy."

"Oh, I am that, a thief and nothing more, Your Honor. Though it grieves me to be saying it," spoke Paddy in an attempt to lend credence to the man's statement.

"You say you work on docks. Now you say you're thief. I say you liar!" barked out Marcos, on striding over to his chair-bound captive.

"And it's stealin' everything I can when I'm there," was the lightning response.

The third party in the room threw back his head in laughter. "The man's priceless!" he roared. It was laughter not shared by his associate.

"I make him tell truth." A hand brushed back the corner of his jacket to reveal a sheathed dagger strapped to the belted pants.

Paddy close his eyes and offered up his first prayer since Communion.

"I say, old boy," spoke the man, "we have business to discuss—in private."

"We go downstairs, then."

"Right. And you can do what you ruddy well want with him when you get back. To quote a certain former Roman administrator, I wash my hands of it."

They then took their leave, but not before Marcos had securely gagged the mouth of his now ashen-faced captive. "You tell truth when I get back, wharf rat," came the ominous threat as deep-set eyes of ocher-brown burned into those of emerald green, "or else . . ." A finger was drawn graphically across the throat from ear to ear.

"But how in the world did you escape?" I blurted out, caught up as I was in his every word and, on noting the houses of Parliament looming into view, desparately hoping to hear the ending before being obliged to alight from the cab.

"What they wouldn't be knowin'," I was informed with a sly little wink, "was that ol' Paddy had a knife of his own. Kept it tucked in me belt at the back. So, there was meself squirming this way and that 'til I got it out and could hack away at the rope. Did you ever try cutting something behind your back you couldn't be seeing?" he asked, displaying a left hand with fingers not without a fine cut or two. "After that," he added, adopting a most casual tone, "it was no more than a minute before I was hightailing it out the window and scooting down the drainpipe."

"Parliament," sang out the cabbie on our arrival.

TWELVE

Descent into Danger

~As we arrived at the House of Commons and entered the gallery out of breath but none the worse for wear, a simultaneous roar of approval followed by much hand clapping arising from the floor below echoed throughout the chamber.

"Is it that well-known, you are, Mrs. Hudson?" asked Paddy.

"I'm afraid it's not for me." I smiled. "It seems our arrival has coincided with that of Lord Salisbury."

"Lord Salisbury?"

"The prime minister."

"So, that's him, is it?" remarked the little man craning his neck round those in the gallery who were now rising to their feet to join in the applause.

With the PM having taken it upon himself to leave his sickbed to put in an appearance in the House, it proved the scene of the deputy prime minister announcing his imminent arrival (as witnessed by Vi while in her astral state) had actually taken place. Not that I doubted for a moment that what she told me was true, or that she at least believed it true, it's just that these ethereal excursions of hers always leave me with a sense of both awe and frustration. Awe at the wonder of it all, and frustration with the multitude of questions that remain unanswered. Be that as it may, it was a matter best left to dwell on at a more opportune time.

As the prime minister stood before his chair, graciously accepting the auditory approval of his colleagues with, I might add, a smattering of tepid hand clapping from across the aisle, my eyes quickly scanned our fellow visitors. "Do you see Marcos?" I asked, knowing he had to be somewhere among the crowd. For, if my theory was correct, he would not have left before actually seeing the PM entering the chamber.

"There!" exclaimed Paddy. "That's himself just behind the lady in the large blue hat."

"The large blue—ah, I see now. Yes, you're right. That's him!" I acknowledged, as my heart began to beat a little faster. I had him. But what was I to do with him? Even if Inspector Lestrade should have burst upon the scene at that very moment, what could he have done? Aside from extradition, the man couldn't be arrested for watching a parliamentary debate. No, he'd have to make the first move. And make it, he did. As he arose from his slouched position in the chair I caught for the first and only time a thin-lipped smile, so confident was he the deed would now at last be carried out. No matter the mangled bodies. No matter the fatherless families that would be left behind. What was it to him? I'd no doubt he'd blow up the world if the price was right. How I hated that man, as well as the one who had engaged him.

"He's slipping out on us again," nudged Paddy.

"Not this time he isn't," I answered. "Quick, now!"

And so began a trail down hallways and stairwells, being always mindful to stay well enough in back of him and thankful for the bustle of bureaucrats popping in and out of doors or traversing the halls in deep and thoughtful countenance as if the very fate of the British Empire rested on their every decision—which, in all likelihood, it did. I also took note and was thankful for the fact that Marcos did not once look behind him. I took this to mean not that he was becoming careless but that he was aware if one marches straight ahead with purposeful stride, he is less likely to be stopped by a watchful guard or an inquisitive politician. As for ourselves? If stopped: an older couple merely seeking out their local MP to lodge a complaint of one sort or another.

Having followed him on his circuitous route, we now found ourselves on the lower level, where, from our vantage point behind a corner pillar, we peered round just in time to see him quickly open and disappear behind an unmarked door. After a pause of a minute or two we cautiously edged our way forward, and on easing open the door discovered to our surprise it led not into a room but to a dimly gaslit staircase leading into the basement.

"Are we going down?" asked Paddy, nervously eyeing the rickety steps descending into the blackness that awaited us at the bottom.

"What would you suggest?" I asked. Then, without waiting for an answer, "Mind yourself, now," I cautioned, "the railing doesn't look all that secure."

After a slow and careful descent we at last reached the bottom, with Paddy remarking in a whispered tone: " 'Tis blacker than a landlord's heart, it is. I'd not be seein' farther than the nose on me face. Are you there, Mrs. Hudson?"

"I'm here. Just a little to the left of you," I whispered back, sure of my bearings by the little man's cinnamon-scented clothing. And while the aroma provided a clue as to his location, in the absence of light the only direction I could now be sure of was up and down. How were we to proceed? I was about to have my answer.

"Would you be lookin' at that now!" exclaimed the bodyless voice beside me.

"What?"

"A light," he answered. Then, "Ah, 'tis gone now. But it was there no more than a second ago or else I'm—"

"No, you're right. I see it now," I was quick to assure him with eyes straining at a distant on-again, off-again flickering of light.

"It wouldn't be the ghost of that Guy Fawkes you were telling me about on the way over, now would it?" he asked with a slight quiver to the voice.

"I think you'll find your ghost is none other than our friend Marcos," I answered. "It would be my guess he has a lantern of some sort that he's either standing or working in front of and as he moves about we sometimes catch a glimpse of light."

"Is that what you're sayin'? But I'd not be remembering him carrying no such lantern on his way down," was the slightly argumentative reply.

"Ah, but remember," I reminded him, "this wouldn't be his first time down here. He's had weeks to plan and prepare for this day."

"It's no doubt you're right," he replied with a smile in his voice, obviously reassured of any fear he had of confronting a specter from the seventeenth century by announcing, "And wasn't it grand of the man to provide us with a beacon of light that'd be leading us straight to him."

That being said, we proceeded silently and surreptitiously through the dark, dank underbelly of the building, with no sounds to be heard save for the constant dripping of water from overhead pipes and the multitude of rats that scurried round our feet. I found myself continuously jabbing at them with the tip of my umbrella though it did but little good.

With eyes becoming somewhat accustomed to the gloom, it was still not enough to tell whether we were wending our way through some sort of storage area or part of the underground heating system though the sound of dripping water would lend credence to the latter. As to our forward trek, it was becoming increasingly frustrating on those occasions when our "guiding" light would suddenly vanish, leaving us to mark time 'til it reappeared. At one point, as we stood waiting in that inky blackness, a rat, taking advantage of stilled feet, began nibbling voraciously at my shoe. I gave it a quick kick, at the same time biting into my hand to stifle a scream.

"Is it alright you are, Mrs. Hudson?"

"A rat," I managed to gasp out, "was trying to make a meal of my foot."

"Ah, now don't you be lettin' these little beggars worry you none," I was advised. "Why, down at the warehouse we got 'em so big we strap kegs to their backs and send them out to the docks for unloadin'."

At any other time I would have laughed; as it was, I simply shuddered as we again moved forward until at last we were able to discern from the light afforded us by the lantern the shape of the man moving about at a distance, I should say, of no more than twenty yards.

"What do we do now?" asked Paddy.

"Move up closer if we can," I advised. "But be careful as well as quiet. We don't—listen," I said, interrupting myself, "do you hear that?" I had caught the sound, which I could only think at the time was that of a low rumbling of thunder.

"I do," he announced after a moment's pause.

We continued to stand in that cesspool of shadows, listening in silence as the sound continued at irregular intervals until it was heard no more.

"I think I might be knowin' what it was," spoke the little Irishman at last.

"You, do? What?"

"You'll be thinkin' I'm a queer one for sayin' it, but it sounded to me like laughter—men's laughter."

"Laughter!" I responded incredulously. "I hardly think—Good Lord, you're right!" It suddenly dawned on me that we had made our way underground to a point just below the chamber. Above our heads sat the British government. Some parliamentary wag from one side of the aisle or the other had, no doubt, injected a cutting remark, producing the deep-throated laughter that had echoed down below.

Marcos had chosen his spot well. With Paddy following close behind, I moved quickly forward. So intent was the man on what he was doing, we found ourselves no more than a few feet in back of him with our presence as yet undetected. I could now see he was attaching wires to some kind of box, a box containing the workings of a clock. This puzzled me somewhat until I realized the man was rigging up a time bomb! As I continued to watch in horrified silence, he suddenly straightened up and, as shoulders tensed, the head, turning ever so slightly, first to the left, then to the right, sniffed the air as would a hound who had caught the fox's scent. Paddy! He had picked up the telltale aroma of the Irishman's cinnamon-scented work clothes.

The creature, for I can think of no other word to describe him, whirled round to see me standing directly in front of him. "You lady I killed on street!" he blurted out, in a face contorted with both shock and puzzlement.

"Not me, you didn't!" I cried. "But this is for Daisy Whyte, the woman you did!" Gripping the middle of my umbrella in both hands, I swung the curved oak wood handle at his head. As his arm came up, shielding the blow, the other lashed out with palm up so that I was literally pushed in the face, with the force of his hand snapping my head back against a wall of brick. As I slid down onto the floor in a sitting position, I suddenly felt myself losing consciousness, with the last sounds heard being those of a scuffle twixt Paddy and my assailant and the ominous tick-tick-ticking of the clock.

"Take a deep breath of air, now. And again. Good. Good." It was the voice of Inspector Lestrade.

"She's coming round, alright. Right as rain she'll be in a minute, you'll see." The voice was Violet's.

What on earth was going on? Was it some sort of dream I was experiencing? In my still somewhat dazed state of mind, I realized I was in a sitting position, and that people seemed to be milling about. As my eyelids flickered open they revealed the faces of Violet, Paddy, and the inspector, hovering over me.

"How is it you're feeling now, Mrs. Hudson?" asked Paddy.

"Didn't I mind you to be careful, Em?" put in Vi. "Thought he'd killed you, we did."

"That's a nasty bump you've got on your head, madam," spoke Lestrade. "But you can be thankful it was nothing more than that."

"I—I don't understand," I stammered, while

bringing myself up into a standing position with an assist from Paddy. "Where am I? What's happened? The bomb!" I suddenly cried out. "Inspector, you must—"

"Never you worry about that, Mrs. Horner."

"Hudson," interjected Vi.

"Yes, well, as I say, never you worry about that. It's all been taken care of," he assured me.

"But, where am I?"

"Why, bless you, luv, you're outside. On the steps," answered Vi.

"Outside? But I was—Will someone please tell me what's going on!" I snapped, angrily brushing aside fallen strands of hair from my face. Standing there in wet shoes, clothes in disarray, and with a pulsating headache just behind my left eye, I felt I had the right to be irritated.

"Well, yes, 'course we will," answered my companion, with a comforting pat to my arm.

"Alright, ladies and gentlemen, move along now, if you please," sang out the inspector to the passing parade of pedestrians who had paused to form a small semicircle around me. "The lady's just had a bit of a fainting spell. Nothing to see. Move along now, that's right."

As they slowly dispersed, with an occasional glance backward, the little Irishman stepped forward. "If you want to be knowin' what happened," he dutifully informed me, "ol' Paddy's your man to tell the tale."

"I'd be much obliged, Mr. O'Ryan,"

"When I sees you slumped down against the wall," he began, "I made me move. Lashed out at him in all directions, I did, with fists flailing away like windmills. But it's sorry I am to say I was no match for the man. Faith now," he went on, heaving a mighty sigh, "if only I'd been twenty years younger and four stone heavier, t'would have been a different story, and that's the truth of it."

"Nevertheless," I was quick to add, "to have attacked him as you did showed considerable courage. And you came to no harm yourself?"

"Just this," he announced, turning his face slightly to the left to reveal a bloodshot eye encircled by a blue-black puffiness to the skin. I drew in my breath at the sight of it. "And haven't I received worse on a Saturday night?" He grinned, in an attempt airily to dismiss the injury, but adding, "Ah, but what wouldn't I have given to have had me old dad's shillelagh with me. Cracked many a skull with it in his day, me old dad did. Mine among them, on more than one occasion I'll be having you know. Black hawthorn it was, Mrs. Hudson, and hard as wood."

"Hawthorn *is* wood," I said.

"Well, there you are now, you see," he answered.

"Yes, well," interjected the man from Scotland Yard, "I think I can take over the story at this point."

"If you would, Inspector."

"When your associate called upon me with her story of a bombing that was to take place within Parliament," he began, as if reading from a report, "I immediately (at the word "immediately" I noticed Vi's face take on a wry expression) set things in motion. Taking my men to the basement below the chamber, where I had reason to believe the deed was to be done (another pantomimed expression of annoyance from Violet who, no doubt, had informed him of our suspicions as to where it would occur) we encountered in that dank underground the sound of someone running toward us. 'Stand where you are!' I cried out, adding: 'Scotland Yard!' That usually does the trick, though not this time, I'm afraid. As Royce here," he went on, indicating one of the men to the back of him, "caught him in the light of his lantern, the man, subsequently identified as Marcos, I might add, drew a revolver from his belt and fired once." He paused, and if it were for dramatic effect, he certainly succeeded.

"Yes, go on," I urged, drinking in his every word. "What happened then? Who did he shoot?"

"Himself, madam. In the head."

I was completely stunned. I couldn't believe it. Everything had happened so quickly. "Marcos—dead?" I managed to utter.

"He is that. Dead as the proverbial doornail, with the body at this very minute being transported to the morgue. Though, that's not to say I wouldn't have preferred to have taken him alive."

"But what of the bomb, Inspector? Obviously it didn't go off. How—"

"Ah, that would be thanks to Jenkins, here," he answered, indicating with a turn of his head a bowler-hatted man off to his right.

"Yes, that's right. Got a bit dicey there for a

second or two," spoke the man, stepping forward.

"That's quite alright, Jenkins, thank you," interjected Lestrade in manner most condescending.

"Right, sir," came the reply with a step backward.

"Now, then," began the inspector, once more returning his attention to me, "leaving the body where it lay, we raced forward to find your Mr. O'Ryan attempting to get you up on your feet. While two of my men assisted you both out to safety, Jenkins made quick work of the mechanics of the bomb, with but a second or two to spare, I might add. And, as the senior man," he added in the grand manner, "I, of course, remained with him to oversee the operation."

"I would have come down myself to lend a helping hand, like," announced Violet, "but the inspector here wouldn't hear of it. For safety sake, he said."

"And quite right he was, too," I stated, adding how thankful I was that any thought of a bombing was now over and done with.

"That part of it at least," acknowledged the inspector. "But the Yard still has a job ahead of it in tracking down the man or men who put him up to it."

I was about to speak when I caught sight of a familiar face coming up the steps toward us.

"Do you know that gentleman?" questioned Lestrade, following my eyes in the direction of the oncoming figure.

"Yes," I nodded, in my surprise. "I know him as Miles Henten of the *Morning Post*. Mr. Churchill designated Mr. Henten as his liaison in our investigation of Marcos."

"Did he indeed, now!" fumed the inspector. "That's all the Yard needs is for the papers to get hold of this before a proper release can be given out."

"I think you can rely on Mr. Henten's discretion in the matter," I assured him.

"I should like to think you're right, Mrs. Hudson," he stated, surprising me by at last remembering my name. "But I've learned one can never be too careful when it comes to dealing with the so-called 'gentlemen of the press.' By the way," he went on, addressing our little triumvirate, "would you three be agreeable to dropping by my office this afternoon? I shall need a statement from each of you. That is, if you feel up to it, Mrs. Hudson. If not, at your earliest convenience. The earlier the better, actually."

"No, that's quite alright, Inspector," I said, much taken by his concern. "I'll be there."

"Are you sure you're up to it, luv?" questioned Vi.

"Perhaps I am still feeling a little woozy," I admitted, "but a bowl of hot broth, a headache powder, and a nap should do the trick. At three, then, Inspector?"

"Three o'clock would be fine, madam."

"Mrs. Hudson, how are you?" spoke the man from the *Post* on his approach. "I had a tip something might be up, so here I am."

"A tip, you say!" thundered Lestrade, ignoring the niceties of an introduction. "It would seem everybody knows what's been going on but the Yard."

"The Yard?" queried the blond giant, looking down at the intense little man staring back up at him.

"This is Inspector Lestrade of Scotland Yard," I informed him.

"Mrs. Hudson tells me that you're in cahoots with Churchill, as well in all this Marcos business. Is that right?" The inspector glowered, displaying obvious displeasure at anyone connected with the fourth estate.

"Well, yes, I am, actually," he stammered. "That is to say—"

"Fine. Then I should like to see you as well in my office at three this afternoon. And," he added quite forcefully, "I don't have to remind you there's to be nothing in the press until you people have clearance from me. Understood?"

"Understood, Inspector," was the dutiful response. "Not a word. Mrs. Hudson" he questioned, turning to me as Lestrade took his leave, "perhaps you could fill me in as to—"

"At three o'clock, Mr. Henten. At three o'clock."

THIRTEEN

The Truth Will Out

꩜ "Yes, do come in, ladies and—Mr. O'Ryan, isn't it?" queried Lestrade as we three made our entrance into the none too large office, to find it even more congested by four chairs sitting semicircle fashion to the front of the inspector's desk.

"It is that, Inspector. Paddy O'Ryan, himself," replied the little Irishman, standing there cap in hand and looking a trifle uneasy.

"If you will . . . ?" The incomplete request was made with a hand indicating the four empty chairs. "You're feeling better now, are you, Mrs. Hudson?" he asked, as we settled ourselves down.

"Much better than this morning, Inspector. Thank you for asking."

"Told her to wait 'til at least tomorrow before she goes out gallivanting again," spoke Violet. "But she'd have none of it."

"Yes, well, we'll try to have this over with as quickly as possible. Just as soon as a certain gentleman from the press shows up we can—ah, speak of the devil," said he, acknowledging a knock on the door. "Come in."

"Sorry I'm late, Inspector," spoke the man from the *Post*, on making his entrance. "But, better late than never, as they say. By the way," he added, withdrawing a writing pad from an inside pocket while slipping into the one remaining chair beside Vi, "would you mind awfully if I took down notes as we go along?"

Lestrade, startled by the request, was quick to follow up his reply with no apparent attempt to hide his annoyance. "Yes, Mr. Henten, I would mind," he snapped. "Royce!" His subordinate, entering from an inner office with note pad at the ready, took his stand to the back of the inspector's desk. "Royce, here, will be taking down all that is said. This is not some sort of news conference I'm holding for your benefit," added the man from Scotland Yard in a most officious manner. "So, if you'll be so kind . . . ? Now, then," he continued, as the pad was obediently replaced inside the pocket, "before we begin, perhaps an introduction or two would be in order. Mrs. Hudson you already know. Seated next to her is Mr. O'Ryan, Mrs. Hudson's how shall we say . . . ?"

"Assistant operative would, I think, best describe Mr. O'Ryan's function, Inspector," I answered.

"Assistant operative," repeated Paddy, with a smile spreading across that elfin face. " 'Tis a grand title, that."

The reporter shifted about somewhat uncomfortably, I thought, before nodding briefly without looking directly at the little Irishman who, in any event, being so puffed-up by the bestowing of his new title, never noticed what could have been construed by some as an intended slight.

"And seated next to you," continued the inspector; "is Mrs. Warner. Mrs. Hudson's associate."

"Pleased to meet you, I'm sure," announced Violet none too convincingly.

"Madam," he acknowledged with another slight nod of the head.

"Now then, sir," spoke Lestrade, "it is my understanding you were asked by Mr. Churchill—make that, Mr. Winston Churchill, Royce," he added in an aside to the man in back of him, "that you were asked," he began again, "to act as some sort of liaison between Mrs. Hudson here and the aforementioned Mr. Churchill, with regard to an investigation he wished carried out on a certain member of the criminal society known only as Marcos. Would that be right so far, Mr. Henten?"

"Right you are, Inspector." He smiled. "And honored I was to have been asked by such a distinguished gentleman. Although, I have to admit that I wasn't as involved as much as I would have liked to have been. What with my work on the paper, I never—"

"Oh, but you *were* involved," I cut in. "In fact, your involvement was an ongoing one, was it not?"

"I—I don't understand," he managed to utter while giving me the oddest look.

"My dear, sir," I began, "don't you think it's

about time you dropped all this pretense? You're not Miles Henten, are you?"

It was a question I posed more as a statement.

"Not—Henten?" came the reply, accompanied by a forced laugh. "Inspector, I do believe the woman's gone slightly senile. Perhaps it might be best," he added on rising, "if a meeting could be arranged between ourselves at a later date."

"If you wouldn't mind returning to your seat, Mr. Henten." Stated casually but with an underlying fiber of authoritativeness, the request was complied with immediately, albeit with a small show of annoyance. "As I have continued to address you as Mr. Henten since your arrival," stated Lestrade, "I take it if it was not your name, I would have stood corrected, would I not?"

"Yes, of course," was the defensive reply.

"The thing is," spoke the inspector, continuing, "at Mrs. Hudson's insistence earlier this morning—make that 'at Mrs. Hudson's request,' Royce: I've seen to it that a certain gentleman drop by who, I'm led to believe, can clear this matter up to everyone's satisfaction. Show him in, would you, Sergeant?" he asked of his subordinate, while looking a little uncomfortable, I thought, as forefinger and thumb began unconsciously massaging the tapered chin, wondering, no doubt, if he'd end up looking the fool in the eyes of the newspaperman if the man should indeed be who he said.

All eyes followed the sergeant as he reopened the inner-office door. "Right this way, sir," spoke Royce to the "gentleman-in-waiting."

"Farnsworth!" exclaimed our "Mr. Henten" as that venerable employee of the *Morning Post* shuffled his way into the room.

"What! Got you down here too, have they? And the ladies as well, I see," he added in recognition of Violet and me. "What's all this nonsense about anyway?" he asked, taking in the man who sat before him in a state of nervous bewilderment.

Before an answer could be given, Inspector Lestrade posed Mr. Farnsworth a question of his own. "Know this gentleman, do you, sir?"

"Know him!" exclaimed the old man, as if it was the most foolish question in the world. "Why, of course I know him. This gentleman is Mr. Charles Ritter. Been with the *Post* a number of years now, he has, though not so many as myself, mind you," he added with a raspy chuckle. "Got yourself into a spot of trouble have you, m'lad?"

At that point, Lestrade once more stepped in to smother the question with a profusion of appreciative responses. "Yes, well, thank you for your time, Mr. Farnsworth. That's all we wanted to know. You've been most helpful indeed," he added, and, with no more than a nod to Royce, the sergeant, acting on cue, escorted the old gentleman to the door.

Ritter. Charles Ritter, I said to myself. At last I had his name. A small victory at best, perhaps, but at least I had justified myself in the eyes of the inspector.

"'Ere," spoke Vi, in a whispered aside, "what's all this Henten-Ritter business, eh?"

"If this mess you've got yourself in involves

the paper in any way, young sir," spoke the *Morning Post*'s head accountant as he turned in parting at the door, "it's best you face up to it now rather than let it end up in court. Best for all concerned—if you get my drift."

"Well, Inspector," smiled the man, exuding a forced show of bravado as his fellow employee took his leave, "it would seem I've been found out. For the horrendous crime of masquerading as Henten, I supose it's 'to the Tower and off with his head' is it?"

"Would that it was," I stated, much to the surprise of all present.

"Obviously," was the inspector's response to my somewhat less than charitable outburst, "you feel that Mr. Hent—Mr. Ritter, that is, has, in some way, impeded your investigation. Perhaps, if you could—"

"Impeded!" I exclaimed. "My dear Inspector Lestrade, he has more than impeded the investigation, he is the *cause* of the investigation."

"What's this you're saying!" cried Lestrade with those beady eyes opening up into little saucers of surprise.

"Not only that," I continued, rising to my feet and pointing an accusatory finger in overly dramatic fashion at the man, "but I have reason to believe that you, Charles Ritter, are an accessory to murder. And that, sir, is just the half of it."

"Murder!" More popping of the eyes from Lestrade who, I surmised, was in fear of what the highly influential newspaper could do to his career should the accusation be proved unfounded.

"Murder!" echoed Violet in equal astonishment.

"I say, this is a bit much, isn't it, Inspector?" voiced the accused, exhibiting an open show of disgust. "I mean, really, old boy, the woman's obviously—"

"Old boy, is it you're saying?" sang out Paddy, who had remained until now silently slunk down in his seat. "*Now* I know where I've heard that voice before. Sure, and it's the same as he who stood to the back of the chair when it was me who'd been bound and gagged by Marcos himself. And that'd be the truth of it."

By now we had all risen from our chairs, with the accused vehemently denying all knowledge of Paddy or of being a party to any murder.

"I think otherwise," I retorted.

"Knew he was up to no good. Told you that from the start, I did," was Violet's contribution to the clamor of rising voices.

"And wasn't it himself who gave me this?" fumed the little Irishman, pointing to a still visible mark on his forehead.

"If you are all quite finished now?" The eyes of the man behind the desk had returned to narrow slits, the face, grim, the voice, low yet commanding. We abruptly halted our recriminations and returned to our seats like so many naughty children.

"It would appear," stated Lestrade, revealing his irritability by the drumming of fingers on his desk, "that I am the only one present who is unaware of certain crimes that have allegedly taken place during your so-called Marcos investigation. An investigation, I might add, instigated and taken part in not by the Yard, mind you, but rather a war correspondent, a newspaperman, a landlady, her companion, and an itinerant dockworker." A sad little shake of the head and a weary sigh followed before I was to come under his gaze. "Since you seem to be the linchpin, shall we say, in all this, Mrs. Hudson," he continued, "perhaps it would be best if we hear from you."

I cleared my throat, took a deep breath, and plunged in. "Since, as they say," I began, "it's always best to start at the beginning, I'll start with my first meeting, as prearranged by Mr. Churchill, with the man I believed at the time to be Miles Henten, outside the offices of the *Morning Post*. As we stood on the pavement engaged in conversation, two men on leaving the newspaper office waved to him. It was after that I was abruptly ushered into a cab, with word he'd see me at a more convenient time. I now know those gentlemen were waving not at Mr. Henten, as I had first thought, but at Mr. Ritter. If they had called out his name in accompaniment with the waving of hands, the jig would have been up. He couldn't chance another such encounter, so off I was sent, posthaste."

Lestrade nodded thoughtfully. "Getting all this, Royce?" he asked. Being assured he was, I was instructed to continue.

"Over the intervening days, indeed, weeks, I had on a number of occasions reason to believe, or at least ponder over, certain things that were either said or done that did not sit right with me in respect to the man I knew as Miles Henten. Mr. Churchill, as did Mr. Farnsworth, spoke of him as a young chap. One would assume from such a description a young man in his early twenties at best. Mr. Ritter here," I added, taking in the haughty face two seats down, "while not old, would I suspect, be a man in his mid-thirties."

"Bless you, dear lady," said he, with a theatrical bow of the head in my direction, adding, "Thirty-seven, actually."

I ignored the mocking response and pressed on. "It was after he visited me at home in the guise of Mr. Henten that I was sure the man I'd been dealing with was not the man he purported himself to be. After we each agreed that the investigation be called off owing to a lack of criminal activity on the part of Marcos—"

" 'Course, we now know the reason why Marcos wasn't up to his old tricks," interjected Violet, feeling a little left out, I'm sure, by my holding center stage, as it were. "He had to wait for the prime minister to show up in the House before he could set the ruddy bomb off," she dutifully informed the ever attentive Lestrade.

"A black-hearted devil he was, Inspector. And who would be knowing that better than meself," added Paddy, if for no other reason than to establish his vocal presence.

"In any event," I continued, "after we had both agreed to drop the investigation Mr. Ritter, as Mr. Henten, offered to send a telegram to Mr. Churchill stating as much, as well as informing Scotland Yard of the presence of Marcos in the city."

"We received no information to that effect. I

should have known about it if we had," commented the inspector. "Royce?"

"We have no record of it as I'm aware of, Inspector," answered the man, dabbing pencil tip to tongue before flipping over to a new page on the pad.

"Exactly," I replied. "Nor was there a telegram sent to Mr. Churchill who, I was to read about the following day, had been captured by the Boers. As a reporter, he would have known about the capture at least the day before the story went to press. Yet he said nothing to me about it."

"I don't wish to sound condescending, Mrs. Hudson," was the sagacious response from the inspector, "but I perhaps have had more dealings with the press than yourself. What I gather from what you've been telling me so far is nothing more than a case of one reporter out to scoop the other man's story. Now, it may not have been ethical in the manner in which he went about it. Nevertheless—"

"Exactly, Inspector!" exclaimed the man, with a self-satisfied smile. "Now, you've got the nub of it."

"Inspector Lestrade," I spoke up in defense, "I'm afraid there's more to it than that. This gentleman was seen in the company of Marcos on three separate occasions."

"Three, you say! Does that include your Mr. O'Ryan's statement of being bound and gagged within the same room as Marcos and Ritter?" he asked, still at odds with himself, I felt, with the believability of Paddy's story.

"It does, Inspector."

"And the other two occasions, then . . . ?"

"The first was during our surveillance of the Tench Street lodgings of Marcos, where Mr. Ritter was seen entering that establishment. His stay was of approximately a half hour's duration," I informed the inspector in what I thought was a very professional manner. Omitting to mention that at the time of our sighting we had no idea it was indeed Charles Ritter. Still, as we now knew, it could have been no other, and since I wasn't under oath . . . "We have, of course, records of the time and date, etc.," I added, turning to my companion. "Vi?"

"What?"

"Our notes," I hissed.

" 'Ere, you didn't tell me you wanted me to bring all that along."

"Yes, well, we can supply you with all detailed memoranda at a more convenient time, Inspector." I smiled weakly, as two little blotches of "embarrassment red" appeared on my cheeks. Nevertheless, I pressed on. "The second occasion was the meeting that took place in a private room at the Blue Boar. As they emerged from the room they found Paddy—Mr. O'Ryan—outside the door. It was at that point that Charles Ritter struck him with a blow to the head."

"Inspector," interrupted the man, "do I have to sit here and listen to all this nonsense?"

"Can you prove any of this, Mrs. Hudson?" asked Lestrade, in an almost pleading tone.

"If you'll look at the cut still visible on Mr. O'Ryan's head and check it with the signet ring the gentleman two seats down is wearing—"

"Looks the same to me it does," sang out Vi, before the ringed finger of the hand resting on the arm of the chair was quickly withdrawn.

"Carry on, Mrs. Hudson," said the inspector, hiding a wisp of a smile, evidently pleased at the way the case was building as thoughts of being castigated by the press began slowly to fade.

I then related to the inspector that being a little late on arriving I was seen, although I didn't know it at the time, by both Marcos and Ritter as they took their leave of the Blue Boar. Marcos, of course, would have no knowledge who I was, but Ritter did. We now had a situation where not only had I been passing along information on Marcos to Ritter believing him to be Henten, but I now show up at the location of what was to have been a secret meeting twixt the two. In order to ensure that a meddlesome old woman not thwart their plan of blowing up the PM and half the government with him, it was decided, probably by Marcos, being the more pragmatic of the two, that I should be done away with. I paused on noting that the sallow face across the desk from me appeared a trifle perplexed.

"Done away with? But, here you are," he said.

"Aye," snapped Vi, "she's here alright, and right glad we are she is. But what of Daisy, eh?"

"Daisy?"

I stepped back in to explain. "Having decided I should be eliminated, our Mr. Ritter would have had to have given Marcos a more detailed description of me, along with my ad-

dress on Baker Street. In one of those unbeliev-
able twists of fate, on the night he approached
my residence out stepped Daisy—Mrs. Whyte,
that is, a neighbor of ours and proprietor of a
shop no more than a block away."

"Always had a smile and a cheery greeting
our Daisy had," announced Violet to no one in
particular.

"Go on, Mrs. Hudson," requested Lestrade.

"Being a woman of my approximate age and
build, she had dropped by to borrow my coat
and hat for an evening out. As she emerged
from the house onto the street, Marcos, believing the woman to be yours truly, followed her
into the fog. Coming up from behind, a hand
reached out, the head was jerked back to expose
the throat, a knife was produced—need I go
on?"

"We do have such a report on file, Inspector,"
stated Royce, taking advantage of a lull within
the room. "If you wish I could—"

"That's quite alright, Sergeant," answered
Lestrade, waving aside the suggestion. "I'm
well aware of the report. What I would like is
to have this Henten fellow from the *Post*
brought in. Since his name keeps cropping up,
it's time we had him down here to hear what
he has to say to all this."

"I'm afraid you won't find Mr. Henten at the
Post, Inspector."

"Oh? You know where he is then, do you,
Mrs. Hudson?"

"No doubt," I answered, steeling myself for
the inevitable response I knew would follow,

"his remains are still at the morgue awaiting identification."

"What! What's this you're saying!" cried Lestrade, completely taken aback by this latest revelation.

"I can explain," I was quick to add.

"I hope you jolly well can!" he fumed. "And if you have any other such information to unveil, I suggest you do it now rather than continuing to dish it out in piecemeal fashion."

Thus, after having been duly reprimanded and, with my added assurance I had no more bodies to offer up—"The thing is, Inspector," I began, "Charles Ritter could hardly continue his masquerade as Miles Henten knowing that sooner or later Henten and I would eventually meet. Indeed, the man must have wondered why I didn't show up at our first meeting when Ritter, as Henten, stopped me outside the offices of the *Morning Post*. I daresay he mentioned to Ritter he'd be dropping by Baker Street to learn the reason why. This, Ritter could not let him do. There was only one way he could carry on his charade, keep his lines of communication open with me, and silence any information his coworker might obtain through his own investigative efforts, and that was by getting rid of him. As my suspicions of Ritter grew, an article Mrs. Warner had pointed out to me in the paper took on added significance."

"The one 'bout that chap drowning?" asked Vi.

"The very one," I replied. "On the one hand, a young man whose body, bearing no identification or identifying marks, save for a mole on the cheek, is found washed up on the banks of the Thames. On the other hand, a young news-paperman involved in an undercover operation remains mysteriously absent from his work. In order to verify my suspicions I had Mrs. Warner check with Mr. Farnsworth for a more detailed description of the missing Miles Henten."

"A well-oiled team, we are, and no mistake," announced Violet.

"And what about meself?" queried Paddy.

"Aye, well, we all know how well oiled you are, Paddy O'Ryan," was my companion's sniggering reply.

"The end result being," I carried on, ignoring the good-natured bantering, "is that verification of the mole-cheeked body of Mr. Henten can be made, I'm sure, either by Mr. Farnsworth or, indeed, any employee of the *Morning Post*, as I understand Mr. Henten had no family."

"You're saying," questioned Lestrade, "it was Marcos and Ritter who did this Henten chap in, then threw the body in the river?"

"I am."

"According to the coroner's report," stated Royce, addressing his superior, "the autopsy did show there was no water found in the lungs. Cause of death was a blow to the head before the body was actually put into the water by a person or persons unknown."

All eyes turned to Charles Ritter.

"Well, this is bloody marvelous, I must say, Inspector," he announced in an all too obvious show of disgust. "According to our female Sherlock Holmes here (I gave him a withering look but said nothing) it seems that not only am I a coconspirator in two murders, but I also stand accused of being the brains behind the plot to blow up Parliament—for which, I have no doubt, this Marcos chap would have demanded quite a sizable fee. Inspector," he added with a hollow laugh, as if to impress the man before him with the absurdity of the accusation, "do you have any idea just how much a reporter, such as myself, makes per annum?"

Lestrade's face sagged.

"There, you see," he continued, adopting a now more confident tone, "the whole thing just won't wash. And as for you, madam," he added, turning to me, "I suggest that in the future you address yourself to the serving of meals and leave the solving of murders to professionals."

"Well, I never!" exclaimed Vi on my behalf.

"That, being said," he announced on rising, "if you have no further need of me, Inspector, I shall take my leave."

"One minute, if you please, Mr. Ritter," I said.

Lestrade's face brightened.

"What is it now, Madam Detective?" was the mocking response.

"A question for the inspector, actually."

"Ask away, Mrs. Hudson," answered Lestrade, while signaling the man to remain where he stood.

"Would I be right," I asked, "in believing a large sum of money was found on the dead man's body?"

"You mean, Marcos?"

"Yes."

"I can answer that there was," stated the inspector a little warily, wondering no doubt where all this was leading.

In truth, I hadn't up 'til now given that much thought to the financial aspect of it all. But as a solution to the puzzle of how an underpaid reporter could finance such a criminal venture began swirling round my brain, I believed, if true, it could swing the onus of the crime once and for all back to Ritter. If I was right—we had him. "Money that he was paid for carrying out his nefarious deed," I stated.

"No doubt it was," replied Lestrade a little wearily. "The question remains, Mrs. Hudson, paid by whom?"

"The answer to that," I stated, "can be found by checking the credit and withdrawal columns of Mr. Ritter's bank records. I believe you'll find the same amount of money in question was transferred by South African sympathizers to Mr. Ritter's account and, the date of withdrawal by him for the same amount for purposes of payment to the late, unlamented Marcos." And, while to me it was only logical to conclude such was the financial arrangement, it was, at best, mere supposition on my part; though I did think the mention of a South African connection added just the right touch of authenticity. Whether I was right in that respect or not, the information provided would, I believed, be enough to warrant an examination of Ritter's financial records by Scotland Yard.

"Inspector," stated the man in no little show of exasperation, "if all it takes to end this farce is a perusal of my account, I'll be glad to bring a statement from the bank over to you personally, first thing tomorrow morning."

He's bluffing, I thought. He had to be, otherwise—

"Tomorrow morning is it, you're saying?" sang out Paddy. "Why, Inspector, the man could be on a ship bound for Tahiti by then."

"Or South Africa, like as not," added Vi.

"Mr. Ritter," began the inspector, weighing each word very carefully, "in light of what I've heard, I find I have no alternative but to have you remain in custody until this whole situation is cleared up to my personal satisfaction."

"Beg pardon, sir, but what would we be booking him on?" questioned the sergeant.

"We do have a choice, don't we?" Lestrade smiled. "Assault and battery should do it for now, I would think."

"I'm thanking you for that, Inspector," announced a beaming Paddy O'Ryan, feeling, I'm sure, vindicated to some extent for injuries received.

So, it was to be assault and battery? The good inspector was playing his cards close to the vest. To have booked a reporter from the *Morning Post* on suspicion of murder and then have it tumble down around him like a house of cards—it was only then did I realize the weight of influence a newspaper has on the Establishment, be it judicial or otherwise. If only the man would confess, I thought—and that's just what he did, though by action, not words.

"See to it that the gentleman is escorted to a holding cell, would you, Sergeant?"

"Right you are, Inspector. Now, sir, if you'll come along with me—"

"I think not!"

The unexpected outburst caught us momentarily by surprise. Charles Ritter made good use of that moment. From his position in back of Vi's chair, he bent over and, in one swift movement, thrust his arm around her throat, jerking her into an upright position. The chair was kicked aside as Vi found herself being dragged backward toward the door. I could do nothing but stand by watching as helplessly as the others as she continued to emit odd little gurgling noises while repeatedly jabbing her elbow into his side. The grip tightened. The jabbing ceased.

"Come to your senses, man!" cried Lestrade, springing up from his chair. "You'll never get out of here!"

"Stand where you are—all of you," he warned, dragging the ever struggling Vi toward the door, "or I'll break her neck!"

"You're only making it worse for yourself, sir," cautioned Royce.

"Oh, I doubt that, Sergeant. Goodbye, one and all," he sang out in one last act of bravado. "If you're ever in the Transvaal, look me up." With that, he released his grip on Violet, shoved her back into the room, and slammed the door behind him.

After but a moment of stunned silence from those of us within the room, Lestrade and the sergeant rushed out into the hallway in quick pursuit. "Stop that man!" cried the inspector, on seeing Ritter make for the stairs. With Royce blowing repeatedly on his whistle, coupled

with the cries of Lestrade and the sound of
heavy-booted feet running to offer assistance,
the man panicked, lost his balance on the top
step, and tumbled forward, landing in crumpled form at the bottom. The sergeant descended the stairs two at a time while we three,
along with the inspector, gazed down over
rail's edge.

"Look," stated Vi, taking in the twisted body
below while unconsciously rubbing a reddened
neck, "he's all bent kinda funny, like."

"The neck's been broken, Inspector," Royce
called up to his superior. "The man's dead."

We made our way silently down the stairs
and, in passing the inert form that lay sprawled
on the floor like a statue toppled from its ped-
estal, I paused for a moment before the man
who was responsible for two murders and, but
for the grace of God, many more, and pondered
the question—why?

FOURTEEN

Reunion

༺ IT WAS IN July of the following
year, the first of the new century, that I, Mrs.
Warner, and Mr. O'Ryan found ourselves listening with rapt attention as Mr. Churchill continued to expound in fascinating detail on his
South African adventures. Having escaped
from his captors and made it back safely to his
own lines, he had become an even bigger hero
to press and public alike. Indeed, on his arrival
back in England his ship was met at dockside
by throngs of cheering admirers. It had been
but a week after his arrival on England's shores
that he took it upon himself to call on me. Only
after our charming raconteur had ended his tale
of military derring-do did the talk turn to the
attempted bomb plot.

It was now my turn to lay the whole story
out before him—with, I might add, assists
along the way by Violet and Paddy—much of
which Mr. Churchill already knew, having spoken earlier to Lestrade. My only regret, as I

mentioned to him in conclusion, was not knowing why Charles Ritter would have been a party
to such an unholy undertaking.

"According to Lestrade," spoke our young
gallant, "an extensive check on Ritter was conducted by the Yard, from which they were able
to piece together an overall picture of the man's
background. It would seem the late, unlamented Charles Ritter was actually born an Afrikaner, having come to England as a small boy
with his parents, the Van Rijks, who were
known in political circles and to the police at
that time as political agitators and members of
various extremist groups. Young Ritter, as I understand it, was treated with complete indifference, at best, by the parents, especially the
father. Yet the lad always looked upon the elder
Van Rijk as some sort of hero. Even though the
boy changed his name from Karl Van Rijk to
Charles Ritter after the death of his parents, his
heart and political persuasions, it seems, were
still on the veldt."

"Then that would explain his motive," I answered thoughtfully. "Having been brought up
in a politically charged environment, he sought
to strike a blow for his homeland by bringing
the South African war to England's shore."

"My thoughts exactly."

"With the plot to blow up the House of Commons," I added, "also serving as a tribute to his
father."

"How so?"

"The boy inside the man was still seeking the
father's approval." Perhaps I had struck a little
"too close to home" as it were, for Mr. Chur-

chill, I thought, shifted about a bit uncomfortably before replying with a noncommittal grunt.

"One thing that don't sit right with me, Mr. Churchill," spoke Vi, as she set about replenishing drinks all around, "is seeing nowt in papers 'bout it. What with bombs and dead bodies and all, I mean, with summat like that, it don't seem right somehow that nowt was said."

"It was the PM's decision to, shall we say, draw the curtain over the whole affair, Mrs. Warner," replied our Mr. Churchill from his stance before the manteled fireplace. "An attempted bombing of the House of Commons that all but narrowly missed in succeeding? You can see how that would have proved to be an embarrassment to the government. And," he continued in a confidential tone, "a word or two from a certain member of the cabinet was enough to convince the *Morning Post* it would be best to quietly let the matter drop."

"Aye," was the resigned sigh from Violet. "Em, here, Mrs. Hudson, that is, thought as how that was the reason. Ain't that right, luv?"

"When one sees in the *Post*"—I smiled knowingly—"articles on the death of two of their staff as being accidental—Miles Henten from drowning and Charles Ritter's demise from a tumble down a flight of stairs—one can only . . . Well, you see what I mean."

"And what would be the story on your lady friend, Mrs. Hudson?" queried Paddy. "Her murder's been covered up as well, has it?"

"You can find Daisy Whyte's death listed on

the police files as an 'unsolved' murder," I answered.

"Well, at least *we* know the truth," proclaimed Violet. "At least that's summat, that is."

"But, then, where," continued Paddy, with a thoughtful scratch to that stubbled chin, "did himself end up?"

"Marcos? I should think," I replied, turning to Mr. Churchill for confirmation, "as an unidentified body in a pauper's grave?"

I received a silent nod in affirmation.

"Sure, and it's like I've always said," spoke the little Irishman, taking it upon himself to empty the remaining decanted sherry into his glass, "you can't be believing half of what you hear nowadays. Would you be agreeing with me or not, Mr. Churchill?"

"The only thing I believe in, Mr. O'Ryan," replied our visitor with an added wink, "is a good cigar. Here," he went on, dipping a hand into an inside pocket, "for you, sir. I have them shipped from Cuba."

"From Cuba, is it now?" beamed Paddy, twirling it lightly round while taking in the pungent aroma. "Ah, it's a darlin' man, you are, sir. But, if you don't mind," he added with a pat to his pocket, "I'll be saving it 'til later."

His benefactor smiled his approval, then, with a glance at his pocket watch and with a clearing of the throat, announced there was an additional reason for his visit. He had been, he stated, requested by both Her Majesty the Queen and the prime minister to extend their heartiest congratulations on a job well-done and to add their deepest regrets that nothing tangible could be offered up in the way of a reward in view of the secrecy that must at all costs be maintained.

The Queen! The prime minister! To say we were stunned by this revelation would be to put it mildly. I remember the remaining minutes of his visit only vaguely, my mind still awhirl. How I wished I could have taken myself upstairs and relayed the news to Mr. Holmes and Dr. Watson. Alas, this I could never do. Somehow I managed to pull myself together and, on seeing my visitor to the door, thought to ask, "And what would be your plans now, Mr. Churchill?"

"I intend to reenter politics, Mrs. Hudson. And this time," he added, with jutting jaw and a determination I had never seen in that boyish face before, "I shall succeed."

"Remember, Paddy," I warned the little Irishman after Mr. Churchill had taken his leave, "not a word to anyone about—you know what."

"There's not a word I'd be sayin', and that's the truth of it," he hastened to assure me.

"Who'd believe him?" remarked Vi, in a quiet aside. "But as for this business of Mr. Churchill going back into politics," she added, "well, I mean, don't the man ever learn?"

"He'd be having my vote, he would," stated Paddy, stoutly defending his newfound friend.

"Why, you great keg-legged sot," was Vi's withering retort, "it'd take no more than a cigar and a handshake for you to vote for the devil himself."

"I take it you're not altogether pleased with Mr. Churchill's decision, Vi."

"Well, I mean, he's not the type, is he? Notice that lisp he has? Fancy him making speeches. He best stick to his writing."

"Is it that sure, you are, Mrs. Warner?" quizzed Paddy.

"Aye," she reiterated. "He'll never make a go of it in politics. I have, what you might call, a sense for things like that. Mrs. Hudson will tell you right enough. Ain't that right, Em?"

In truth, I thought the young man possessed a commanding presence and an indomitable spirit that would see him through whatever path he chose and whatever pitfalls that lay ahead. Still, with it being a victory celebration of sorts and not wishing to sound a note of discord with my companion, my only recourse to her answer lay in a noncommittal reply.

"If that's what you believe, my dear, Mrs. Warner," I announced, smiling sweetly, "who am I to argue?"

ANN GRANGER

The Meredith and Markby Mysteries

"The author has a good feel for understated humor, a nice ear for dialogue, and a quietly introspective heroine."

London Times Saturday Review

COLD IN THE EARTH	72213-5/$5.50 US
A FINE PLACE FOR DEATH	72573-8/$5.50 US
MURDER AMONG US	72476-6/$5.50 US
SAY IT WITH POISON	71823-5/$5.50 US
A SEASON FOR MURDER	71997-5/$4.99 US
WHERE OLD BONES LIE	72477-4/$4.99 US